Women of the Word

VOL. 1

Melissa Joy Parcels

WOMEN OF THE WORD
VOL. 1

iUniverse books may be ordered through booksellers or by contacting:

iUniverse
1663 Liberty Drive
Bloomington, IN 47403
www.iuniverse.com
844-349-9409

Because of the dynamic nature of the Internet, any web addresses or links contained in this book may have changed since publication and may no longer be valid. The views expressed in this work are solely those of the author and do not necessarily reflect the views of the publisher, and the publisher hereby disclaims any responsibility for them.

Any people depicted in stock imagery provided by Getty Images are models, and such images are being used for illustrative purposes only. Certain stock imagery © Getty Images.

Scripture quotations marked NIV are taken from the Holy Bible, New International Version®. NIV®. Copyright © 1973, 1978, 1984 by International Bible Society. Used by permission of Zondervan. All rights reserved. [Biblica]

ISBN: 978-1-6632-3977-8 (sc)
ISBN: 978-1-6632-3978-5 (hc)
ISBN: 978-1-6632-3974-7 (e)

Library of Congress Control Number: 2022908785

Print information available on the last page.

iUniverse rev. date: 06/09/2022

Contents

Dedication

To Jesus, who gave me new life, and Papa, my Heavenly Father, who loves me with an everlasting love.

To my mother, Krista, who raised me to love the Lord.

To my sister, Ashley, who taught me the redemptive power of Jesus and his measure of incredible love.

Introduction

The Lord has given me a passion to teach the Bible and inspire others to live a decided life for Christ. I hope the reader will learn about the lives, decisions, and outcomes of these women in the Bible and grow deeper in their love and understanding of God's character and truth.

This book is designed for a personal journey with Jesus. You can read this alone or invite women to join you in a group setting or in a Bible group within your church. It includes outlines, discussion questions, prayers, and declarations.

The Challenge to the Reader

The goal of this book is to give you a practical guide through the women of the word, their Bible passages, and stories. You must read things carefully, go into the scriptures, and allow the Holy Spirit to teach you things for yourself. The time for passive Bible learning is over. This is the call to action! You're here to make a difference and to learn God's character truly and fully within your spirit, then go and make disciples.

Each week, approach the reading with an open mind and an open heart. Allow God to teach you things in new ways. As you study these women, I hope that you will see things within yourselves, both good and bad, that you can surrender to God. We can all grow in love, conviction, and faith.

Answering the Probing Questions

This book is also a workbook equipped with questions and sources for scripture that allow you to unpack the content in your own time. These questions can also be used in a Bible study group to share and engage with others.

Open Heart Posture

As you read this book, I desire that you walk by faith. Allow the teaching of Jesus to come through the stories of these women. Let it change you. Allow the truth to mold your character to look like Christ. Within each woman's story you have a takeaway that does just that.

Enjoy reading *Women of the Word*.

Melissa J Parcels

Acknowledgments

I would like to thank God first and foremost. I needed Your grace and loving hand that guided me through the writing of this book. You are a good father.

I thank Jesus. Thank You for leaving the ninety-nine to pursue my prodigal heart. I am so glad You gave me new life; I love You and owe You everything. May everything I do give You glory.

Thank you, Holy Spirit, for Your guidance and teaching as I put my vision to paper. You have strengthened me and taught me things each step of the way. I am grateful for Your leadership.

I thank Ryan, my husband. You have always been a support to me and my ideas, and you have been a part of this book at each step. Thank you for once again being right by my side.

I thank my son Kesler. You were still in my womb while I wrote this book, and it was the promise of you that sealed my heart in love and motivation. Thank you for being a constant joy for me.

I thank Stella, a dear friend who has been faithful, honest, true, and supportive during the writing of this book and Bible classes—you have never missed one!

I would like to thank my friends, whom I affectionately call the B team. Your prayers and support while hosting classes have been so appreciated—I love you greatly.

I thank Dara, my editor. You edited this book with grace and meticulous detail, and I appreciate your great talent and editing eye. It was God who arranged our partnership, and He never fails to be faithful.

Weekly Format

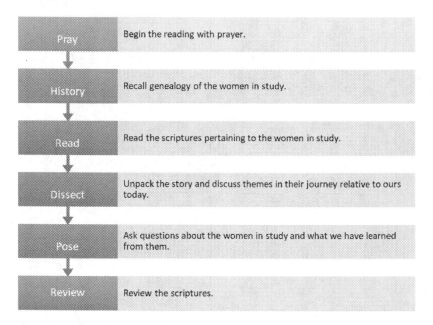

Pray — Begin the reading with prayer.

History — Recall genealogy of the women in study.

Read — Read the scriptures pertaining to the women in study.

Dissect — Unpack the story and discuss themes in their journey relative to ours today.

Pose — Ask questions about the women in study and what we have learned from them.

Review — Review the scriptures.

WOW Week One

Prayer:

Lord, open our eyes and ears to receive Your word today. Let all distractions be eliminated, and allow our hearts to be focused on You and what You want to deposit in our spirits today. Let our lives give You glory. Amen.

This week we will study the lives of Hagar and Lot's wife.

The Chosen Line in Genesis

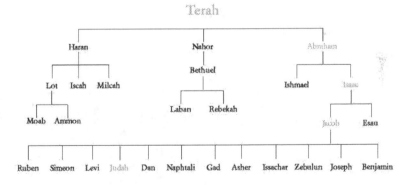

This chart indicates the chosen line found in the Book of Genesis.
The names in blue are the lineage of the Messiah.

Bible History Online

1

Hagar

A woman who was met by God

Hagar was Abraham and Sarah's Egyptian slave. Because Sarai (Sarah) and Abraham had not had children during the ten years they lived in Canaan, Sarah gave Hagar to her husband to sleep with and marry. Hagar did not have a choice. She was told what to do and had to obey.

Sarah's decision to give Hagar to her husband to be a surrogate womb was made in the flesh as she was able. She was trying to solve the problem of an heir for her husband on her own without God's instruction. Abraham did not consult God on the matter either; rather, he listened to Sarah's plan and followed through. This decision was man's response to a problem. Sarah was determined to fix it on her own. She was not depending on God. She was impatient and doubted God's ability to work in her life and womb.

Hagar had sexual relations with Abraham (probably regularly to conceive) and became pregnant. After this, in any encounter Hagar had with Sarah, Sarah was harsh and cold because of jealousy. The ugly spirit of jealousy can ruin a good relationship and cause major division in our lives if we allow it to take root as Sarah did. Hagar ran away because she was feeling hurt and unappreciated. While in the desert, an angel of the Lord visited her by a spring or well and told her that she should not avoid Sarah. He confirmed that she was pregnant with a son and that the Lord's grace was upon her for what she had endured. The angel told her to name her son Ishmael. He would be wild in character, but a legacy to many nations. She felt saved and redeemed.

It is believed that that the angel of the Lord may have been Jesus Christ incarnate to meet Hagar in her despair. He came to meet her extreme need. She cried out for God to save her in the wilderness at the oasis that didn't offer her rest. Jesus was her way to deliverance. In humility and repentance, she obeyed Him and turned back to Abraham's camp. Obedience is always rewarded. *Read 1 Peter 5:6–7.*

Hagar's sin, like that of Eve, had been pride. Renouncing her spirit of pride and rebellion, Hagar returned to Sarah, her mistress. Hagar did the opposite of acting in pride, she abased herself—she humbled, lowered, demoted, and reduced herself. God can use the humble at heart, not the proud.

God looked after Hagar because He understood her suffering. Hagar went through unnecessary pain because Sarah disobeyed God's plan to wait for Him. After Hagar's return to the camp, another angel visited Abraham and told him that Sarah herself would also have a son. From inside a nearby tent, Sarah overheard and laughed at the idea, being as she was ninety years old and long past childbearing years. The Lord kept His word, however, and Sarah did have a son. She named him Isaac, which means "laughter" or "the one who laughs." Even though Sarah had doubted God's ability to fulfill His promise, God still kept His unchanging word to her.

In the lineage thereafter, Ishmael became the Persian bloodline, whereas Isaac, the inheritance to Abraham, became the Jewish bloodline. These exist to this day, and there is still a war between them.

There are subtle parts in the Word that reveal negative attitudes between Hagar and Sarah, with Hagar treating Sarah disrepectfully once she conceived. Sarah responded in an angry manner to Hagar looking down on her.

According to the law, Abraham was not able to approach Hagar himself; it had to be done through Sarah. Nor was it Abraham's idea.

All three were responsible for trespassing God's laws and were equally guilty. Hagar couldn't take the constant harassment of Sarah, now that she was pregnant. She fled into the wilderness without permission, knowing that it might kill her and the baby. Even Hagar's name means "flight."

When Isaac was about three years old, Ishmael was an older teenager, approximately seventeen. There was a celebration to honor Isaac, and he was getting praise and attention in the camp that Ishmael didn't like. He began to mock his younger brother out of jealousy (Genesis 21:9). Ishmael felt second to the son of promise, Isaac. He may have been unaware of the promise over his own life in the wilderness with his mother many years before. Not knowing the promise over Isaac's life, he refused to accept a subservient position to a younger brother.

Sarah saw Hagar's son, Ishmael, as a mockery to their family name. She believed her son was the rightful heir. She was correct; God gave her Isaac as the legitimate heir of the promise. Sarah told Abraham to send Hagar and Ishmael away, and this, of course, caused Abraham great distress. He had been a good father to his son Ishmael for seventeen years, and he loved his sons equally. Nonetheless, Abraham knew the division in his family would not get better unless Hagar and Ishmael were gone. He prayed about this, and God revealed through prayer that the separation of his sons was necessary. The line of prophecy and inheritance of the tribe of God and the people of Israel would be through Isaac. He alone was the son of promise. He would become the forefather of the family of the twelve tribes of Israel. God assured Abraham that both his sons would have many descendants. God instructed Abraham to listen to Sarah and assured him that He would keep Hagar and Ishmael safe in the wilderness.

After this revelation (revealed truth) from God, Abraham came to understand why Isaac was so important and that Sarah was right. But, like Isaac, Ishmael would also become a forefather of a family of twelve tribes because he was the son of Abraham. After years together as a family, Abraham listened to Sarah and sent Hagar and Ishmael away in the wilderness. Hagar started into the desert again. The physical journey was hard, with blistering heat and distance, and they didn't have enough food and water for this long journey into the unknown. Eventually, they ran out of water, and Ishmael was too weak to walk. Hagar placed him under a shrub and went a short distance away, unable to bear watching her son die. She began to sob. The same voice from nearly twenty years prior spoke to her and said, "Do not be afraid." Her son would be taken care of and later would become the leader of a great nation. At that moment, a fresh wellspring of water appeared. She and her son drank in new life.

Now we see that Jesus had come a second time to save her and her son from certain death in the wilderness. Years later, Hagar went to Egypt and got a wife for her son. Unfortunately, this was not in obedience to God, who wished for Abraham's descendants to marry God-fearing

6

spouses. The Lord she had called on to help her in her life had sadly not become Lord *of* her life. Because Hagar did not obey God's laws, the conflict between her son and Isaac went on to affect the entire world.

Ishmael, who lived to be 137 years old, went on to be the father of the Arab nations, while Isaac became the father of the Jewish nation as the one true promise child. To this day there is still animosity between these two groups. It's a very explosive relationship. This is an example of generational curses and sin and how destructive disobedience can be to God's plan. It shows us the consequence of sin. Read more on the blessings and curses in Deuteronomy 28.

Initially, Hagar suffered the consequences of someone else's—Sarah's—sin. If we examine our own lives, we can also see the consequences of other people's sins. And perhaps other people have suffered because of our sin. God knows the end from the beginning, and His ways and thoughts are higher than ours. *Read Isaiah 55:8–9.*

Even though a human's flawed decision affected the story, God was faithful to carry out His ultimate plan and to continue to make all things come together and work for good for those who love Him.

Verses about Hagar:

> ➢ Genesis 12:1–5; 15:2–5; 17:5–16; 16:7–12; 21:22–23; 25:12–16
> ➢ Exodus 3:2–6
> ➢ Judges 6:11–23
> ➢ James 2:23
> ➢ John 4:4–42; 8:3–11
> ➢ Philippians 2:5–11
> ➢ 1 Peter 5:6

Questions about Hagar:

1. What have you learned from Hagar's struggles about the Lord's character?
2. Have you ever experienced God's intervention in your life? Can you share the details?
3. Do you have a great understanding of the impact of your sin?

Fill in the blanks (use the English Standard Version [ESV] translation):

Genesis 16:11. "The angel of the LORD also said to her: "You are _____and will give _____to a _____. You shall name him _____ for the Lord has heard your misery."

Genesis 16:15–16. "So, Hagar bore _____ a son, and Abram gave the name _____ to the son she had borne. Abram was _____old when Hagar bore him Ishmael."

Personal reflections:

Read 1 Peter 5:6–7. What does the Bible say about our attitudes?

_____

_____

Do you trust God when things do not go your way?

_____

_____

Have you been ruled by jealousy of other women and trapped in comparison that you can repent for?

_____

_____

What does the Bible say about our uniqueness?

_____

_____

Lot's Wife

A woman who disobeyed God's warning

Read Genesis 19:1–7. This passage talks about two angels who came down to confront the sin in Sodom. There was rampant idol worship, violence, and sexual sin taking place in the city at the time. The Lord was coming to warn Lot, an honorable man to God, and his family before He burned the city down in righteous judgment.

The two angels came to Lot's house. The people in the city came demanding the men be brought out as they wanted to have sex with them. Lot offered his virgin daughters instead of the angels, as he knew the two were from God and hospitality was tremendously important in that culture. This upset Lot's wife, and in hindsight it was a terrible fatherly decision.

When the men of the city attempted to break into Lot's house, the angels struck the men with blindness, then told Lot to gather his family and leave Sodom immediately as they were going to destroy the city. Read Genesis 19:24–26.

This passage of scripture talks about the rain of fire that God poured on Sodom and Gomorrah as Lot's family was escaping. The only instructions the angels had given were, "Don't look back, look ahead, and run into the mountains"

(Genesis 19:15–17 NIV). But Lot's wife did look back at the lost city and immediately turned into a pillar of salt. There is a salt stone there today, mildly resembling a women's body, that tour guides say is Lot's wife. To this day, tourists from all over the world come to the site of Sodom and Gomorrah and the nearby "Sea of Lot," known more commonly as the Dead Sea. Sodom, in the present-day, is a barren landscape; nothing grows there. Centuries earlier, it had been a land full of green life.

Did Lot's wife know that the men with her husband were angels? That they had investigated the city to see how wicked it had become? Probably not. She probably did not know that Abraham had been praying for Sodom, and God had agreed to spare her family as a result. Lot's wife did know, however, how evil the city was. She had lived there for years, seeing the wickedness and ungodly things happening, and how the city inhabitants did not live for truth. But she had continued to live there and did not want to leave. When the angels told her and Lot to leave the city, she may have even thought to herself, *Why should I leave my home?* She was more concerned about Lot's honorable position in the city as a wealthy man, and her easy access to worldly goods when compared with how life had been with Abraham in the wilderness. She was a person who desired worldly affirmation. She possessed a spirit of rebellion and independence.

The city of Sodom had become so corrupt and infiltrated with the spirit of the false god Baal and sexual sin. The men in the city even wanted to rape other men who were visiting. The city was plagued with sexual immorality. It was unclean and "vile" in our Heavenly Father's eyes, but that didn't seem to matter to Lot's wife.

In the New Testament passage Jude 7, the writer comments on how Sodom was a city that "indulged in gross immorality," and in 2 Peter 2:6 (NIV) it reads that "Sodom was reduced to ashes." We can understand that Lot's wife became upset with Lot when he offered their daughters to the men of the city for sex before their escape. She may have been too upset to listen to the angels for instruction on when and how to leave. She may not have believed that they were sent to save Lot. But after the angels blinded the mob of people to help them escape, she surely started to believe. Both Lot and his wife began to obey their instructions.

Some things in scripture remain unknown: how she and Lot met, and if she had roots in Sodom; her background and even her name are mysteries. The Bible does not say whether she had a personal relationship with God. She was close to Sarah and Abraham, who spoke of God, so there's little doubt that she had been introduced to God and His laws through interaction with them.

Lot did have a relationship with God at some point, but as he lived in Sodom, he became more lukewarm and distant from God. This shows us that if our environments, relationships, workplaces, etc., are not godly, they can become a barrier to our relationship with God and even draw us away from Him. God, despite His anger towards Sodom, still spared Lot's family. God had grace for them. Lot's wife doubted this grace. She wasted time. She looked back, longing for the sinful city instead of being grateful for God's mercy.

Even though Lot had recently become distant from the Lord, God still considered him a righteous man. God always looks at the heart of people. As they were hesitating to leave the city, the angels grabbed their hands and ran with them. "Flee for your lives! Don't look back, and don't stop anywhere in the plain! Flee to the mountains or you will be swept away" (Genesis 19:17 NIV).

When God wiped out Sodom and Gomorrah, there was not a blade of grass left. When God's judgment rained down on the place that held the heart of Lot's wife, she disobeyed the angels' command and looked back. She physically left Sodom, but her heart was still there. Her looking back sealed her fate; it was her doom, her demise. Her doubt in God and longing for the things of this world was what killed her. She could have escaped death and lived with her family in the mountains or the small town of Zoar where Lot initially went.

Jesus later uses her example as a warning. In Ephesians 2:6 Jesus said, "Remember what happened to Lot's wife?" Given final judgment, He was teaching His disciples of the final judgment still to come. Lot's wife was sealed in doom, but her story can be a blessing to others if we learn from it. The story of accepting God's grace can save others. Scripture says, "So we must listen very carefully to the truths we have heard, or we may drift away from them" (Hebrews 2:1 NIV).

Lot's wife Bible verses:

> ➤ Genesis 13:10; 17:4-5, 18:20–21, 23–33; 19:12-15 Psalms 28:5
> ➤ Isaiah 26:10
> ➤ Luke 17:32
> ➤ Romans 1:26–27
> ➤ 2 Corinthians 6:1
> ➤ Ephesians 1:7–8; 2:8
> ➤ Hebrews 2:1–3
> ➤ 2 Peter 2:8

Questions about Lot's wife:

1. What was the Sodomite's major sin according to the Bible passages? "Sodomites" is a word derived from the biblical town of Sodom,. Which was heavily laden with connotations of homosexual immorality.
2. In your opinion, what was the sin that cost Lot's wife her life?
3. What was your big takeaway from the story of Lot's unnamed wife?

Fill in the blanks (use the ESV translation)

Genesis 19:29: "But Lot's wife _____, and she became a _____ of salt."

Genesis 19:17: "And as they brought them out, one said, "_____ for your life. Do not look back or stop anywhere in the valley. Escape to the _____, lest you be _____ away."

Genesis 19:13: "For we are about to _____ this place, because the _____ against its people has become great before the Lᴏʀᴅ, and the Lᴏʀᴅ has _____ to destroy it."

Personal reflections:

Why do you think God asked Abraham to pray for Sodom?

_____

_____

Why do you think Lot's wife turned back?

_____

_____

What does Romans 5:19 say about disobedience and righteousness?

_____

_____

Are there areas in your own life where you are being disobedient to God? Name them and repent, asking the Holy Spirit for help.

_____

_____

Week One Review

Review your Bible verses for each woman. Pray for new revelation from the word.

Weekly Challenge:

Ask God to search your heart for any rebellion or independent attitudes toward His instruction for you.

Prayer:

Heavenly Father, I ask You to uproot any rebellious seeds in me that stand against Your will. I want Your will over my own. Help me take direction well and be obedient to Your voice. Allow the Holy Spirit to help me as I walk out my salvation. I ask to have learned from Hagar and Lot's wife what not to do in situations where I cannot see the outcome. Help me to trust You completely. I surrender my heart to You, Lord. In Jesus's name, amen.

Weekly Declaration:

I declare I have the grace I need for today. That with God nothing I face this coming week will be too much for me. I will overcome all obstacles and outlast every challenge through the blood of Jesus. I am an overcomer. This is my declaration.

WOW Week Two

Prayer:

Lord, I come before Your throne of grace boldly asking to be changed by Your word, to allow transformation to take root in my heart according to Your will. Open my eyes and ears to respond to Your truth in Your scriptures. In Jesus's name, amen.

This week we will study the lives of Rachel, Abishag, and Dinah.

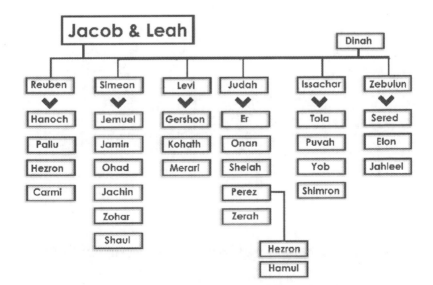

Rachel

A woman whose jealousy destroyed her ability to enjoy God's blessings

Genesis 29:1–30 outlines the story of when Jacob met Rachel and Leah. He was tending the field of his mother's brother, and when he saw Rachel, he fell in love with her beauty. She was a shepherdess and his first cousin (relationships like this between cousins was not uncommon in the culture). Because he fell in love with her, he wanted Rachel as his wife instead of wages for his fieldwork. *Read Genesis 29:16–30.*

When Rachel saw Jacob roll the stone away in the field, she was amazed. There was something familiar about him that she was attracted to. She realized it was her cousin, the son of her father's sister, Rebekah. Rebekah had moved away many years before to marry Isaac. Jacob said he would work for seven years to earn Rachel's hand in marriage. So he and Laban, Rachel's father, made a deal. Jacob was faithful to his work; he did it well and did not complain. He was so in love with Rachel that the seven years seemed but a few days to him.

After seven years, the day had arrived when he was going to marry Rachel and then likely leave to go back home to start his life with his new wife. However, Laban tricked

Jacob into marrying his eldest daughter, Leah. When Jacob realized the next morning that he was married to the wrong woman, he was confused, angry, and felt deceived. He reminded Laban that his seven years of serving had been for Rachel, not Leah.

Laban explained his deception by explaining that it was not the custom in their culture to marry off the younger sister before the eldest was married. He had to "marry off" Leah, who was not as beautiful. He said, "Finish this daughter's bridal week, then we will give you the younger one also in return for another seven years of work" (Genesis 29:27 NIV). Jacob agreed. He married Rachel a week later. Laban gave both the women female servants. Jacob remained on the land for another seven years with both sisters as his wives, working for Laban.

When Jacob declared his love for Rachel and requested that her hand in marriage be his payment for working for Laban, the Bible never tells us what Rachel's reaction was to this. It doesn't mention her feelings about what happened at what was supposed to have been her wedding, either, which likely was very painful. Laban was deceitful. He didn't care what he had to do if the end worked out well for him. He used the emotions Jacob had for Rachel to get free labor for seven years and used them again to get an extra seven years of work by tricking Jacob into marrying his less attractive daughter. As a result, it would no longer be his problem to try to marry her off.

There is no record in the Bible of Rachel's reaction to her father's deception. Did her outward beauty also resemble in her heart? Did she hurt for the pain of the man who had worked for her for seven years? A week after Jacob married and bed Leah, he married Rachel. The tension was high between the wives, especially because they were sisters. The fact that Jacob did not love Leah made matters worse.

Leah took this need that wasn't being met by her husband who did not love her to the Lord. She was desperate for Him and His heavenly comfort. Because of this, God opened her womb with six sons and a daughter.

Leah might not have had outward beauty, but her inner beauty was growing and shining. Rachel reacted differently. Because of her poor character, it did not leave room in her heart for her to be grateful for her husband's love or compassion toward Leah. Her heart grew cold. God closed Rachel's womb. At this point, she did not have any children with Jacob. Rachel felt privileged over Leah, entitled because he loved her. Rachel became jealous of Leah's motherly happiness. She demanded of Jacob, "Give me children or I'll die!" (Genesis 20:1 NIV). These words caused deep pain in his heart. He knew that Rachel preferred death over the shame of being barren, which in that culture was considered a curse. Rachel's statement not only dishonored her husband—as if he had intentionally prevented her from having children while giving them to Leah—but also dishonored God. Rachel's pain of barrenness didn't drive her into God's arms as Leah's pain of loneliness did.

Rachel felt as if she competed with Leah. It was a contest to her—another example of sibling rivalry like that of Cain and Abel. Rachel lived in a land where the custom was that if the wife could not have children, she could give her servant as a concubine to have children on her behalf and then claim them as her own. So Rachel brought a concubine into the marriage, and it complicated things that were already complicated. God's design for marriage was one man and one woman to be unified as one flesh in marriage. In the case of marriage, more is not merrier.

When Rachel's servant, Bilhah, gave birth to a son, Rachel named the baby Dan and said, "God had vindicated me.

He has listened to my plea and given me a son" (Genesis 30:6 NIV). This gives us great insight into her mindset and character. Although she said it was God who did this, it had been her own manipulation. She was using this event to compete with Leah and finally felt vindicated and justified. She wasn't. She had responded in the flesh and settled her issue on her terms without seeking God first.

Years passed, yet Rachel's jealousy remained in her heart. Rachel did not know the meaning of true love. Leah's firstborn son, Reuben, was in the field one day and found a mandrake root that was considered to increase fertility. Rachel demanded the son give her the fruit. She told Leah that if the boy would give her the fruit, Jacob could spend the night with Leah. Out of this night's union, another son was conceived between Leah and Jacob.

We must remember that human self-love will not rob God of His deserved majesty. God loved Rachel even though she was not beautiful on the inside. God had a soft spot for Rachel's struggle. God allowed her to conceive a son, and she named him Joseph. Even after God gave her a son, she remained jealous and seemingly ungrateful. Her situation changed but it didn't change her heart. "Give me, give me" was her repeated life stance. Sadly, she remained unchanged by God's goodness.

After Joseph was born, Jacob heard the Lord tell him to move back to his homeland with his wives and children and to set roots down in Canaan. He told both Leah and Rachel together. This would be the first time they had left their home village to start a new life. Even though Jacob was close to God, Rachel didn't come close to God or have a personal relationship with Him. Rachel became immersed in pagan idols from her father. Rachel put her trust in these idols, whereas Leah, who also grew up with these idols, chose to trust God.

Before they left on their journey, Rachel decided to steal her father's sacred idols and keep them for herself. She did this in secret. She did not tell Jacob, her husband, what she did, which shows that they did not have a deep enough intimacy for her to share her burdens with him. Laban was very angry that the items were stolen and he blamed Jacob. Jacob said he would execute anyone who had taken the idols, and told Laban to go ahead and search for them himself because he was convinced they weren't there. Rachel's father checked the people's belongings and did not find them. Rachel had hidden them in a satchel that she was reclining on. She claimed to have her period and didn't feel well enough to get up. The idols were concealed and never discovered. She was as deceitful as her father had been (Genesis 31:31-36 NIV).

God talks many times, from Genesis to Revelation, about the contents of a man's heart. He knows that human hearts are selfish, evil, wicked, and full of pride. "The heart is deceitful above all things and beyond cure. Who can understand it?" (Jeremiah 17:9 NIV). We cannot change our hearts on our own; only God can do that through our surrender and repentance. Therefore, in our prayers, we must surrender and answer God's call: "Give me your heart and let your eyes delight in my ways" (Proverbs 23:26 NIV). We must have Him continually search our hearts as David asked of the Lord.

God's love has to penetrate our hearts, and we must surrender our pride and allow God to make changes starting from the inside out. Rachel's prideful heart created blockages in her heart that hardened her. Rachel's frustrations about her life and motherhood did not result in a joy-filled life. She did get pregnant again by God's grace, but she died while giving birth to another son. In her last breath, she named her son Ben-oni, which means "son of my sorrow." Jacob renamed him Benjamin, "son of my right hand" (Genesis 35:16-19 NIV).

Joseph (Rachel's first son with Jacob) was young when she died but grew up to become a great man of God, consistent and trusting of God. God destined him to become an extraordinary blessing to the Hebrew people with an amazing journey. Of the twelve tribes of Jacob, Rachel's sons, both Joseph and Benjamin, were among them, along with the two sons of Rachel's servant, two sons from Leah's servant, and the six sons of Leah. Jacob did favor Rachel's sons over Leah's. Shortly after Rachel's death, Jacob renewed his covenant with God.

Verses about Rachel:

> Genesis 29:15; 30:1–6, 33, 35; 31:14–16
> Deuteronomy 8:8, 16
> Jeremiah 17:9–10; 5:23
> Proverbs 16:5; 23:26
> Hebrews 12:15

Questions about Rachel:

1. What have you learned about the human heart and its innate response to things?
2. What does the Bible reveal about the heart of Rachel when it came to her marriage and her sister?
3. Do you see any blessings from God in Rachel's life?
4. How could Rachel have made a positive contribution and influenced her family history positively instead of negatively?

Fill in the blanks (use the ESV translation):

Genesis 29:31: "When the LORD saw that Leah was _____, he _____her womb, but Rachel was _____."

Genesis 30:22: "Then God remembered Rachel, and God _____to her and opened her womb.

Genesis 35:24: "The sons of Rachel: _____ and _____."

Proverbs 3:6: "In all your _____acknowledge him, and he will make _____your paths."

Personal reflections:

Name two verses in the Bible that discuss the heart.

    1. _____
    2. _____

Do you ask God to search your own heart while in prayer? If not, why?

_____

_____

Name one example in your life when you received God's mercy and grace when you did not deserve it.

_____

What does this story teach us about Jesus's Sermon on the Mount and the truth about spiritual poverty?

_____

_____

_____

Abishag

A woman who served her king

Abishag (ab-ish-hag) is a beautiful story laid out in 1 Kings. *Read 1 Kings 1:1–4.* Abishag was a Shunammite woman who lived about thirty hours away from the capital city where King David's palace was. King David was advanced in years and quite frail. Nothing—not the fire, not his clothes—kept him warm at night, so his advisor suggested a woman might help keep him warm. His advisors traveled the Israel coast. They had to search and search for a suitable virgin for their king.

They finally found Abishag of the Issachar tribe. She would have been about sixteen years old, living at home, unmarried. Abishag was a very important example of "surrender" that the Bible gives us. She was in search of her significance. Many times, in our current society, we search for significance; we want to matter. This thinking can lead us down a road of self will over God's will for our lives.

When Abishag was summoned by the king, she had to decide what to do. She had to surrender many things for the call of this service. This cost her a lot. She surrendered her life, family, friends, and plans for a normal marriage with children to move far away and live in an unknown place. She surrendered her freedom.

Psalm 134:1-3 NIV says "minister" before the Lord in service. She would have to give her life in service of what the king needed. She was King David's concubine although they were not intimate; she was still the property of the king even after his death. This meant she couldn't marry and have a family of her own. In biblical times, having children was a way of gaining significance, having worth; she gave this up for duty.

It says in 1 Kings 1:2 NIV that Abishag was beautiful. She probably already had suitors for marriage. But Abishag stood in service to the king, surrendering the plans she had for her life. We all have plans, wants, desires, things we want to accomplish and experience. It would have been no different for her. We must ask ourselves if God asked us, would we surrender our plans to Him, trusting His will? That part of our Christian walk can be a process. It says in 1 Kings that she was to cherish King David, although he did not know her. Cherish means to have feelings for. She had to make up her mind to serve God and her king, then allow feelings to follow. *Read Proverbs 16:3–4.*

God is asking for you to commit to Him, whether feelings are there or not. He wants your obedience, even over your sacrifice. In 1 Kings 2, we see the significance of her surrender again. Before King David dies, his fourth son, Adonijah (his son with Haggith), has plans along with his mother to be king and take David's place. However, King David's desire and the will of God was for Solomon, David's tenth son, to be the next king. King David said, "no" to Adonijah, but Adonijah schemed by asking for Abishag to be his wife. He knew that she was the property of the king and therefore was significant to the throne. By marrying her, that would have placed him first as king in the people's eyes.

Satan will always try to lie to you and say things like, "If you give God everything, He will forget you and you'll be left with nothing." I am sure he tried this with Abishag, making her believe she was just a pawn in a political game. Abishag might have felt like she didn't matter. At times, like in the story of Abishag, when we question our significance and obedience to God in our thoughts, we must remember what Paul said in Romans. *Read Romans 12:1–2.*

Abishag was a great example of serving God with her body, her will, and later her feelings by cherishing King David. Even though her role was relatively small, her story teaches us that we all are positioned for greatness inside God's plan, and in His great compassion for us, He allows us to choose to be part of His plan. The king's advisors scoured the kingdom for one who would serve with "no questions asked" and didn't find anyone until Abishag. May we learn to lead as she did and by her example see what God can do with a heart willing to serve.

Verses about Abishag:

➤ 1 Kings 1:1–4, 15; 2:17, 21–22Psalm 134:1–3
➤ Romans 12:1

Questions about Abishag:

1. Has God asked you to surrender something of great significance that was difficult at the time, but later you saw why His will called for surrender?
2. What was something you took away from the story of Abishag?
3. What did Abishag's obedience reveal in your own life?

Fill in the blanks (use the ESV translation):

1 Kings 1:1. "Now King David was old and _____ in years. And although they covered him with clothes, he could not get _____."

1 Kings 1:3. "So they sought for a _____ young woman throughout all the _____ of Israel and found Abishag, the _____, and brought her to the king."

Personal reflections:

Have you said no to serving when God called you to some area?

_____

Do you bring Jesus obedience over sacrifice?

_____

Write 1 Peter 4:8 and what this means to you.

_____

_____

_____

What areas in your life does this story show you that you need to grow in?

_____

Dinah

A girl whose curiosity led to destruction

In Genesis, it says Dinah was the daughter of Leah and Jacob, his only one. Dinah's life consisted of simple day-to-day tasks and little "new" conversation. She did not have many people to talk to other than her mother, brothers, and servants. Every few months or years, they were on the move again. They were making their way back to Canaan where her father, Jacob, wanted to eventually settle and put down roots. *Read Genesis 30:21–34 and 46:15.*

"After Jacob came from Paddan Aram, he arrived safely at the city of Shechem in Canaan and camped within sight of the city. For a hundred pieces of silver, he bought from the sons of Hamor, the father of Shechem, the plot of ground where he pitched his tent" (Genesis 33:18–19 NIV). Dinah was longing for something more than a life of traveling in tents, though. She was restless. She wanted to meet other girls who lived in Shechem, a city close by. So one day, Dinah left her parental tent and began walking to Shechem. The Bible never tells us if her parents knew she had left camp to visit Shechem

When she arrived in the city, the young Prince Shechem, named after the city, saw her and lusted after her. He desired her and raped her. But he also fell in love with her.

He asked Jacob for her hand in marriage, but when Jacob learned what the prince had done, defiling his daughter before marriage, he was angry. The Bible never tells us details of the assault; we do not know if she tried to escape. But it was a horrible, dishonorable crime and when Dinah's brothers found out they were furious.

Surprisingly, Prince Shechem still wanted to marry her. A wealthy prince, he asked Jacob to name the dowry price for her hand in marriage. Simon and Levi (two of Dinah's brothers) demanded that the prince and his men in the city all get circumcised, saying it was a command of God. They knew the prince could not marry her because he wasn't circumcised, but it was a ploy to cover their revenge plot. Prince Shechem was popular and well adored in the city and truly had plans to marry Dinah, so the men of the city agreed, believing that they would be able to intermarry with the tribe of Jacob and thus increase their wealth.

The brothers pretended that they were OK with Shechem marrying their sister, but in reality, they had made other plans to kill the men and plunder the city of Shechem. The men from the city were still in pain from their circumcisions. Dinah's brothers came and killed Hamor, Shechem's father, and Shechem for defiling their sister. Then they murdered all the men of the city. But even this wasn't enough to satisfy their hatred, so they robbed the people of the city and took their flocks, sheep, donkeys, and household wealth. They even kidnapped the women and children.

After the massacre, the word spread about Levi and Simeon. What they had done on account of revenge hurt Dinah and Jacob's family name. Jacob said, "You have brought trouble on me by making me obnoxious to the Canaanite and Perizzites." (Genesis 34:30 NIV). God's name was so closely connected to Jacob's name that God's name suffered too. Jacob's attitude toward his two sons was one of rebuke. The rape and massacre grieved God and brought the family great shame in the region and among other people in the area. After this, God commanded Jacob to move his family away to Bethel. *Read Romans 12:19.*

The seemingly innocent trip to a new city for adventure turned into chaos and a righteous family's disgrace. Dinah's departure from the family tent to find friends and adventure turned into an unfortunate crime and brought shame and sorrow into her life. Like all women who have experienced rape, she was never going to be the same; something was taken from her that only God could replace.

The Bible doesn't mention anything about Dinah after this or how Jacob treated her. Did she get attention and love from her father? Was she ever able to marry? We don't know.

Leah's response to the events that unfolded is not mentioned in scripture either. We can suspect Leah might have been comforting to her daughter, personally knowing the pain of unfortunate life events and the consequences of other people's choices. God does not always stop bad things from happening to us, but He does weep with us when they do.

Verses about Dinah:

> ➤ Genesis 31:18; 33:18–20; 34:30; 28:19–22; 31:33; 12:14–20; 26:7–11; 32:28–29
> ➤ Deuteronomy 22:20–21
> ➤ Proverbs 3:12

Questions about Dinah:

1. List some obvious consequences of Dinah's trip to Shechem.
2. Why (in your opinion) does God place such high value on virginity?
3. Why must we not take vengeance into our own hands and give it over to the Lord?
4. Explain the actions in this story of jealousy and how God handled it.

Fill in the blanks (use the ESV translation):

1 Corinthians 6:9–10. "Or do you not know that the _____will not inherit the kingdom of God? Do not be deceived: neither the _____, nor idolaters, nor adulterers, nor men who practice homosexuality, nor _____, nor the _____, nor drunkards, nor revilers, nor swindlers will inherit the _____ of God."

Genesis 34:1: "Now _____the daughter of Leah, whom she had borne to Jacob, went out to see the women of the _____."

Personal reflections:

Do you identify with Dinah's adventurous nature, which may have opened doors to sin in your life as a result?

_____

Who in the Bible can make our crooked paths straight?

_____

We have all experienced injustice in our lives. What does the Bible say about the topic and from whom should we seek justice?

_____

_____

_____

Why do you think Jacob was shamed by his sons' actions? Do you think they got fair punishment?

_____

_____

Week Two Review

Review your Bible verses for each woman. Pray over new revelation through the word.

Weekly Challenge:

Ask God to search your heart for any anger or desire to get even that you may have toward anyone. Ask God to bring opportunities to bless another person this week.

Prayer:

Heavenly Father, I come before Your throne of grace as a sinner wanting to be more like Jesus. I ask You to continually show me my sin and help me repent quickly and desire holiness and righteousness, the way You have defined them. Let my life speak the fruits of the spirit. I know You go ahead of me and prepare a way, and I trust You, Jesus. I want my life to depend on You and your truth because, Jesus, You are the way, the truth, and the life. Have Your way in my heart today, Lord, in the name of Jesus I pray, amen.

Weekly Declaration:

I declare that God is going before me to prepare a place. According to His trusted word, God makes crooked paths straight and is before and behind me. He will line up the right conversations and relationships, open the doors for me this week, and allow opportunities for sharing the gospel. No person, roadblock, or enemy attack will stop God's plan in my life. What He has promised will come to pass. This is my declaration.

WOW Week Three

Prayer: Lord, I trust You with my time. I know You go before me and prepare a way. I ask You to prepare a way today for Your truth to take root in my heart. Let this word nourish me and grow me as I walk out of my salvation with You at my right hand. I trust You and love You, Lord, in Jesus's name, amen.

This week we will study the lives off Tamar, Hannah, and Deborah.

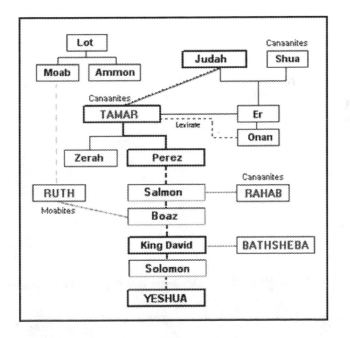

Tamar

An overlooked woman who was vindicated

Read Genesis 38:6–12. Judah, Leah's son, had three sons of his own: Er and Onan and Shelah. Judah found his eldest son, Er, a wife named Tamar (tay-mar). Er was wicked in the Lord's sight, though, so the Lord put him to death.

In that culture, the law was that if your daughter-in-law was a widow, you must find her a new husband in your family. The law required Onan, Er's brother, to marry and give offspring to his widowed sister-in-law.

Judah asked Onan to go to Tamar and impregnate her to allow the family bloodline to continue. Onan was upset by this since any child that would be born would not legally be his heir. He wasted his sperm during intercourse with Tamar. The Bible says he "spilled his seed on the ground" (Genesis 38:9 NIV). The Lord was displeased with this and took his life too. The next statement in the Bible says that Onan did "evil" and that God slew him. God cut Onan's life short for his disobedience.

God had promised that the Messiah would come from the tribe of Judah. Judah said Tamar would have to wait until his youngest son, Shelah, was grown; then he would give her in marriage to him. Until then, she had to live as a widow, mourning her husband and wearing mourning clothes.

Years passed. Tamar felt that Judah was not going to keep his word since Shelah had grown up but she had not been given to him in marriage. Judah probably deemed Tamar to be cursed because both of his sons had died by God's hand prematurely after marrying her. Likely, he never intended to follow through on his word to marry Shelah to Tamar. A few years later, Judah himself became a widower and made plans to go to a nearby city to shear his sheep at a festival. Tamar found out that Judah was coming and disguised herself as a prostitute on the side of the road. She hid behind a veil so Judah could not recognize her.

Tamar planned to become pregnant by this ruse so that she might bear a child in Judah's line. Since Judah had not given her to his son Shelah as promised, she took the matter into her own hands. She played the part of a prostitute and struck a bargain with Judah to have intercourse with him for the payment of a goat. (This was the usual payment offered for sexual deeds. It would be sacrificed later at the altar of the fertility god or goddess to whom the prostitutes often dedicated themselves in an act of witchcraft.) Judah did not have the goat on hand; after shearing his sheep he would be able to pay her. So she secured his staff, seal, and cord until he paid the debt. But when Judah was later able to have a goat sent to collect his staff and seal, the woman was nowhere to be found.

Read Genesis 38:12. The villagers said there was no prostitute in Timnath. Judah had not allowed God to guide his actions. Now he feared what he had done. He certainly would be humiliated if word got around that he was consorting with prostitutes. He decided he would just forget about it and move on. Three months later, Judah learned that Tamar was pregnant, obviously because of her having unlawful sex. Tamar was then accused of prostitution. Upon hearing this news, Judah ordered that she be burned to death (Genesis 38:24 NIV). This was a violent response, even in that culture; especially from our perspective, considering that he had visited a prostitute himself. Could this be a result of his underlying hatred for her over the death of his sons?

Judah's judgment of Tamar was ruthless. Tamar had suffered plenty, losing two husbands, unable to bear children, living as a widow. But now he had sentenced her to death. He said, "Bring her out and burn her" (Genesis 38:24 NIV). This statement does not exhibit grace or the love of the father's heart. Remember how Jesus responded to the prostitute in the New Testament? He responded with mercy.

When Tamar arrived at the place of accusation, she was calm, however. She knew she had the ticket to keep her life. She presented the personal items Judah had given her and said the owner of this staff and seal was the father of her unborn child. When Judah saw the items, he recognized them and knew they were his. He was appalled. His sin was exposed, and very publicly. He couldn't conceal it any longer. Judah released Tamar from her sentence.

Read Numbers 32:23. Judah had to admit what he had done, that he had not kept his promise to her and fulfilled her legal rights. His public reply in the matter was, "She is more righteous than I since I wouldn't give her to my son Shelah, and he did not sleep with her again" (Genesis 38:26 NIV). Tamar secured her place in the family as well as Judah's posterity. She gave birth to twins, Perez and Zerah. Their birth is reminiscent of the birth of Rebekah's twin sons. The midwife marked Zerah's hand with a scarlet cord when he first emerged from the womb, but then he pulled it back and Perez was born first. Perez is identified in the Book of Ruth as the ancestor of King David. *Read Ruth 4:18–22.*

Tamar's intentions were resolute. She knew what she wanted. She had weighed out the consequences of her actions, knowing the cost could be high. When Christ came, He was not afraid to expose sin and to love us in a correction. Christ came to show that He loves people and was not afraid to connect with those caught in sin. Later, Matthew wrote the genealogy of Jesus, a long list of mostly men; only five women were named. Tamar was the first one. Her son, Perez, was in the lineage of Jesus. God saw her heart.

Read Romans 8:29. Christ did something very special for women while he was here on earth. He gave them back their position and value. He gave them back their rightful place where God intended them to be before Eve's fall in the garden. He treated all women with respectful love. He nailed unfair treatment of women to the cross. Tamar's story only gains perspective when the light of Jesus shines on it. Jesus extended the honor to her of becoming a mother in the early history of His earthly family.

Verses about Tamar:

> ➢ Genesis 3:16–17; 38:8, 24–25; 49:8–10; 38:11
> ➢ Matthew 1:1–17
> ➢ John 8:3–10
> ➢ Hebrews 13:14

Questions about Tamar:

1. Explain why you think God did not forget about Tamar.
2. Who are the five women that are in the lineage of Christ?
3. Do two wrongs make a right?
4. What was the number one principle that you took away from the story of Tamar?

Fill in the blanks (use the ESV translation):

Genesis 38:11. "Judah then said to his _____ Tamar, 'Live as a widow in your father's household until my son _____ grows up.' For he thought, 'He may _____ too, just like his brothers.' So Tamar went to live in her father's household."

Genesis 38:26. "Judah _____ them and said, 'She is more _____ than I, since I wouldn't give her to my son Shelah.' And he did not _____ with her again."

Personal reflections:

What does the Bible say about premature death?

_____

_____

When God says Israelites prostitute themselves, what does He mean?

_____

_____

Speaking honestly, would you have humbled yourself and admitted your sin as Judah did or would you have denied it?

_____

Write Psalm 24:3-5 and reflect on the verses in this passage.

_____

_____

Hannah

A woman who bargained with God

Hannah is a woman in the word who is famous simply for her prayers, but as we unpack her life, we see there is so much more to her story. Hannah had a heart that was genuine and honest with the Lord, and we know from His word that He looks at the heart. *Read 1 Samuel 16:7.*

The story of Hannah comes from 1 Samuel 1:1–28 and 2:11. She was married into the tribe of Ephraim. Her husband was Elkanah (El-can-uh) and he had two wives, Peninnah and Hannah. It is recorded that Hannah had no children. Her sister-wife, however, had many children. In that culture, women received their value from having children, especially sons.

Without children, they were not considered worthy. This was the case for Hannah. Although her husband loved her, her sister-wife was cruel and mean to Hannah. Hannah's barrenness made her sad and introverted and brought her to be more reliant on God.

Annually, their family would travel to the town where the tabernacle was to worship and make a sacrifice to the Lord. The priest Eli was there with his two sons to run the service. Elkanah would offer his sacrifice and then would give a double portion of meat to Hannah because he loved her. But he only gave a single portion of meat to Peninnah. This would have been insulting to Peninnah. Having borne Elkanah's sons and daughters, she thought she was well deserving of the double portion. Sometimes we do not understand why people are blessed, and that can lead to the sin of jealousy. Year after year, Peninnah would mock and degrade Hannah to the point of tears.

Hannah felt so unfilled, so desperate, that she prayed and pleaded with God during her duress. We see from the scriptures that she didn't confront Peninnah, tell her off, blame her husband, or even stand up for herself and refuse to be bullied. She didn't do any of that; we read in the chapter that she drew near to God.

We must remember that in our worst times when we have been unjustifiably treated poorly, we must pour our hearts out to God, cry to Him, and allow Him to heal and avenge our pain. *Read Leviticus 19:18.*

Hannah showed such humility and honor to God to behave in a way that would please the Lord. In her heart, she knew only God could change her circumstances. She knew it wasn't her husband's problem, for he was able to have children. The problem was within her own body. Hannah prayed to God and even made a bargain with God that if He would give her a son, she would dedicate that son back to the Lord to do His work. This is the first time in the Bible we see bargaining with God, and we read that when it came time for Hannah's miracle, God remembered her.

God sometimes allows people to be blessed whom we don't think to deserve the blessing. And sometimes those we think should be blessed are overlooked. What we see in the life of Hannah, however, is that even with the cards she was dealt (and being so persecuted and taunted), didn't turn her away from God; it made her run toward Him. Something most women wouldn't have handled well actually created a steadfast nature in Hannah.

God was planning to do something incredible with her life, and therefore a time of wilderness was needed to test her spirit. We see these tests many times throughout the Bible and even in the life of Jesus. God created a complete dependence on Him and purified the heart through the fires of tough circumstances.

Read Malachi 3:3. Hannah could endure something that was beyond her control to change. She was a great example of "hanging tough." She didn't fight back with negativity on how she was treated. *Read 1 Samuel 1:7.*

Can we, for a moment, put ourselves in Hannah's shoes? Have you longed for something that was not given naturally? Can you imagine what it was like to also have a sister-wife publicly degrade your worth year after year? How very difficult that would be. Hannah had the fortitude to "take a licking and keep on ticking," one pastor has said.

Hannah also didn't use her circumstances to drive her to devices such as sin, drinking, or negative outbursts. We see Christians today often allow their circumstances or past pain to drive them to sin instead of propelling them into purpose. God is asking us to search our hearts to make sure we desire the Lord more than the job we want, the children we want, or any desires for things more than the Creator. True blessing comes when we let go and release our unknown outcome to God. He is the finisher of our faith. We can see that Hannah didn't use the justification of her drama to allow a sinful nature to form; she resisted and ran to God. She had an honorable heart and pleaded with the Lord for a son.

God sees your dilemma, like He saw Hannah's. Her approach was to plead with and seek the Lord. Her prayer became famous because it was her seeking that changed the Lord's heart and put her in remembrance with Him. We know that Peninnah had many children, yet she did not have compassion for people who struggled or for people lacking what she had in abundance. In our prayer life, we should ask God to search our hearts and create in us pure hearts that see people who are struggling or doing without. May the Lord birth in us a desire to bless others in ways He directs us.

Eli saw Hannah praying at the temple, but she wasn't speaking out loud, and he thought she was drunk. But she told him, "I am a woman who is deeply troubled. I have not been drinking ... I am pouring out my soul to the Lord" (1 Samuel 1:15 NIV). Eli blessed her and prayed that the Lord would hear her cry. He did. Hannah had a son and named him Samuel. He would become the great prophet and last judge of the Old Testament, an incredible instrument of God used by Him to further establish His kingdom on earth. When God delivered Hannah from her trouble, He went above and beyond, as God often does.

Hannah had promised God to give her son back to the Lord in service. So, after he was weaned at about four years old, she brought him to Eli to be trained as a priest of the Lord. She dedicated him back to God, like we dedicate our children to God today. In Chapter 2, we see her famous thankful prayer for what God has achieved in and through her life and how He changed her circumstances. She went on to have five more children.

Verses about Hannah:

> ➤ 1 Samuel 1:1–28, 2:1-11
> ➤ Psalm 119:50

Questions about Hannah:

1. Do you have an attitude like Hannah in your current circumstances? Or like Peninnah, who was self-focused?
2. In troubled times, do you run to God and seek His comfort and wisdom?
3. Is there a time in your life when you saw God's provision and promises return so much bigger than you imagined or even asked for?
4. Is there someone in your life who is like Peninnah that you can love and show compassion to?

Fill in the blanks (use the ESV translation):

1 Samuel 2:20: "Then Eli would bless _____ and his wife, and say, 'May the LORD give you _____ by this woman for the _____ she asked of the LORD.' So, then they would return to their home."

1 Samuel 2:21: "Indeed the _____ visited Hannah, and she _____ and bore three sons and two daughters. And the young man _____ grew in the presence of the LORD."

Personal reflections:

What can I learn and apply to my own heart from the life of Hannah?

_____

_____

Why is my dependency on God so important to Him?

_____

_____

What does the Bible say about the treatment of those who mistreat us?

_____

Write out Romans 8:18 and what it means to you.

_____

Deborah

A faithful leader of a nation who stepped up in a time of need

God raised Deborah to the position of "judge" of her people, in part because the men didn't want to step up. This was the highest political position in the land at the time. There was no king.

She was alive approximately thirteen centuries before Christ. It has been said that in history very few women have obtained the public dignity and supreme authority that Deborah did.

She would later be known as the "Mother of Israel" and her faith led the way for Israel's faith. She was a mediator for her people, a judge at the time of a dispute, and a war leader in times of battle. She was a woman of excellence. She became a great leader in her time because she trusted God completely. She could inspire others with that same trust.

At that time, the king of Hazor (a country neighboring Israel) was an evil man named Jabin. His general was also a wicked man named Sisera. Together, they destroyed the vineyards of the Israelites, raped their women, and killed their children. At the time, Israel was heavily involved in idol worship and witchcraft.

Deborah was from a land of olive trees and palm trees. She would sit under a palm tree and give counsel to people who traveled for her wisdom, but her greatest achievement would be in a time of war. Her people were oppressed, and this injustice lit a fire in Deborah's heart. Her spirit was fearless. The people she led were afraid because the nation against them had nine hundred chariots and they had none. Deborah was not afraid; she knew the Lord was with her.

She knew that God would come to the rescue of her people in battle if they would come to honor Him in their lives and stop their idol worship. She was faith driven. The men in her time would not lead; they were afraid. Deborah called them out and denounced the lack of leadership. She rose as a willing leader for her people. Because of her zeal and passion, God armed her with new strength and endurance. She was a heroine; she had spirit in her voice, passion in her step, and fire in her eyes. From humble beginnings as a housewife, God raised her to unite a nation and lead it into victory as a powerful woman of God.

She found an army general named Barak and summoned him. She told him about the plan she had been given by God for victory over Jabin's army. She told Barak that they would win against this army. He was humble of heart, and he needed her counsel and faith. He sensed her spiritual insight and agreed to her plan.

He said to her, "If you go with me, I will go. If you do not go with me, I will not go." It is a very insightful passage in the Bible, as it says a military man had so much confidence in a woman that he did not want to go to war without her. This was not common in that culture. What was it about

Deborah, the homemaker, that made people want to follow her and trust her? It was her unwavering faith in God.

Deborah was also a prophetess. A prophet or prophetess is a person who is in contact with the divine, serving as a messenger for humanity and delivering messages and teachings from the supernatural source, God. Deborah told Barak she would go with him. But because of Barak's fearfulness, God would deliver Sisera, Jabin's general, into the hands of a woman, not to Barak himself.

On the day that God would deliver Sisera into a woman's hands, the Israelites stood with ten thousand warriors but no chariots. Deborah and Barak went up to a rock and she explained to him the battle strategy.

It says in Judges 5 that the heavens poured out the rain (likely hail and sleet) on the faces of Sisera and his army. Can you imagine their swordsmen crippled by the cold and the archers disarmed by the hail? The river started to flood so badly (verse 21), the charioteers washed away. All Sisera's troops fell by Israelite swords. Sisera himself ran for his life and abandoned the battle. He ran to the tent of a woman named Jael. Her husband was an ally of Jabin, so Sisera thought he would be safe (Judges 4:18-21 NIV).

Jael welcomed him into the tent and gave him warm milk and lodging. He quickly fell fast asleep. While he was asleep, however, she took a tent peg from the ground and hammered it through his temple and killed him. When Barak came looking for Sisera, Jael took him and showed him the dead body. It was just as Deborah had prophesied: Sisera would be drawn into—killed by—the hands of a woman.

Deborah was praised for her leadership and prophesying. She gave all the glory to God. Her devotion to her people and their freedom can be heard in the song dedicated to her in Judges 5. Her people were no longer enslaved. Her victory was the final freedom for Israel. It reads in Judges 5:31b: "Then the land had peace for forty years." When Deborah first started, the younger people had never known freedom. It was a word that their parents had only spoken of.

In the years before the time of Deborah, there had been a level of peace as the good judge Ehud led the people to serve God. But when he died, the Israelites fell back into worshiping idols and sin came into their hearts, so God "sold them into the hands of Jabin … who cruelly oppressed the Israelites for twenty years" (Judges 4:2–4 NIV).

Deborah was one of twelve judges spanning the time between Joshua and Samuel, the last judge before Saul was anointed the first king of Israel. Because of the oppression of Jabin, the roads were deserted, and evil was everywhere (Judges 5:6 NIV). People went to Deborah to judge their disputes and she gave them direction for their lives. *Read Judges 4:1–5.*

Joshua and Samuel were not officially of the twelve judges, but Samuel is portrayed as a judge and leads the military in the book of Judges. He also exercised judicial functions. Like the other judges, Deborah was appointed by God to bring her people back to a relationship with God. Deborah and Barak fought together and worked on their plan for the defeat of Sisera. Between them there was never competition or comparison of skills; they worked as one unit for God. Deborah said to Barak, "Rise up." She allowed this to be an encouragement to him that this battle isn't between them and Sisera, but God and Sisera.

Read Judges 4:12–24. God moved on their behalf and caused a storm, which made Sisera's army weak and rendered them ineffective. Barak's army was able to have victory for God. Since the beginning of time, God has decreed that men and women should complement each other, like in marriage. Women and men are created equal, but with different gifts. The partnership of man and women are completed in marriage. Barak and Deborah demonstrated this harmony in their partnership.

God is not always looking for a man to take on leadership. In this story, it was a woman, and it was a matter of the heart. It always is with God. If you want in your heart to be used by God, He can use you and work in you and through you greatly. Deborah did not take the glory for herself; she gave it to God. She simply described herself as the mother of Israel. As a mother who looks after the well-being of her children, she looked after the well-being of her people.

Song of Deborah—**Judges 5 (NIV)**

[12]Wake up, wake up, Deborah!
  Wake up, wake up, break out in song!
Arise, Barak!
  Take captive your captives, son of Abinoam.'

[13] "The remnant of the nobles came down;
  the people of the LORD came down to me against the mighty.
[14] Some came from Ephraim, whose roots were in Amalek;
  Benjamin was with the people who followed you.
From Makir captains came down,
  from Zebulun those who bear a commander's[c] staff.
[15] The princes of Issachar were with Deborah;
  yes, Issachar was with Barak,
  sent under his command into the valley.
In the districts of Reuben
  there was much searching of heart.

[16]Why did you stay among the sheep pens[d]
  to hear the whistling for the flocks?
In the districts of Reuben
  there was much searching of heart.
[17] Gilead stayed beyond the Jordan.
  And Dan, why did he linger by the ships?
Asher remained on the coast
  and stayed in his coves.
[18] The people of Zebulun risked their very lives;
  so did Naphtali on the terraced fields.

[19] "Kings came, they fought,
  the kings of Canaan fought.
At Taanach, by the waters of Megiddo,
  they took no plunder of silver.

[20]From the heavens the stars fought,
  from their courses they fought against Sisera.
[21] The river Kishon swept them away,
  the age-old river, the river Kishon.
  March on, my soul; be strong!
[22] Then thundered the horses' hooves—
  galloping, galloping go his mighty steeds.
[23] 'Curse Meroz,' said the angel of the LORD.
  'Curse its people bitterly,
because they did not come to help the LORD,
  to help the LORD against the mighty.'

²⁴"Most blessed of women be Jael,
the wife of Heber the Kenite,
most blessed of tent-dwelling women.
²⁵ He asked for water, and she gave him milk;
in a bowl fit for nobles she brought him curdled milk.
²⁶ Her hand reached for the tent peg,
her right hand for the workman's hammer.
She struck Sisera, she crushed his head,
she shattered and pierced his temple.
²⁷ At her feet he sank,
he fell; there he lay.
At her feet he sank, he fell;
where he sank, there he fell—dead.

²⁸ "Through the window peered Sisera's mother;
behind the lattice she cried out,
'Why is his chariot so long in coming?
Why is the clatter of his chariots delayed?'

²⁹The wisest of her ladies answer her;
indeed, she keeps saying to herself,
³⁰ 'Are they not finding and dividing the spoils:
a woman or two for each man,
colorful garments as plunder for Sisera,
colorful garments embroidered,
highly embroidered garments for my neck—
all this as plunder?'

³¹ "So may all your enemies perish, Lord!
But may all who love you be like the sun
when it rises in its strength."

Then the land had peace forty years.

Verses about Deborah:

- ➤ Genesis 1:26–28
- ➤ Judges 4:3–7, 9, 14, 16, 17–21; 5:1–3, 31
- ➤ Proverbs 4:18
- ➤ Ecclesiastes 8:5
- ➤ Isaiah 40:31
- ➤ Hebrews 4:6–7

Questions about Deborah

1. How well do you think Deborah did working with Barak?
2. How much did she focus on God over herself? Do any examples come to mind?
3. Do you have an example of how God used a woman to make a difference in His kingdom?
4. What is your big takeaway from the story of Deborah?

Fill in the blanks (use the ESV translation):

Judges 5:24: "Blessed above women shall _____the wife of Heber the Kenite be, blessed she be above women in the _____."

Judges 5:26: "She sent her _____ to the tent peg and her right hand to the _____; she struck Sisera; she crushed his head; she shattered and _____ his _____."

Personal reflections:

What does God say about women in leadership?

_____

Do I have God-honoring friendships with the opposite sex?

_____

Write Psalm 11:21 out and reflect.

_____

_____

_____

Do you believe Jael was used by God in His perfect timing to execute judgment on Sisera? Do you know God as both merciful and righteous in His judgments?

_____

Where does my faith measure up in comparison to Deborah's faith, knowing the battle was already won for her?

_____

_____

Week Three Review

Review your Bible verses for each woman. Pray over new revelation through the word.

Weekly Challenge:

Ask God to awaken boldness in you. Challenge yourself to be bold in conversations and opportunities to share the gospel.

Prayer:

Heavenly Father, I come before Your throne of grace asking You to equip me in areas that help me advance Your kingdom. I want to be a vessel of honor to You and have my life be an example to others of Your goodness and faithfulness. Help me walk with the Holy Spirit and learn from His voice and conviction. Remove distractions in my life and blinders from my eyes so that I may see Your way and know Your truth more clearly. Allow my heart to respond to the Holy Spirit with obedience and trust. Lord, I want to put You first in my life. I want to know You fully and have a relationship and fellowship with You. Sharpen me in areas I need to be sharpened. I ask You to send people into my life that need to see Your goodness so that I can show your love to them. I humble myself before You, Lord. I desire Your will for my life. In Jesus's name, I pray, amen.

Weekly Declaration:

I declare a great legacy of faith over my life. I declare with my life to honor to God, knowing this will store up blessings for future generations in my bloodline. My life is marked by God's goodness. Because I am choosing the godly way to live, people I know will follow my example. God's goodness will follow me all the days of my life. This is my declaration.

WOW Week Four

Prayer: Lord, I trust You with my time. Allow the voice of the Holy Spirit to lead me today as I unpack Your scriptures. Let seeds of purity and righteousness take root in my heart. Let the Holy Spirit teach me, convict me, and transform me into the nature of Christ so I can bear His fruit. In Jesus's name, amen.

This week we will study the lives of Delilah, Naomi, Zipporah, and Ruth.

There was tension and war between the Philistines and the Israelites. The Philistines often invaded their land.

Delilah

A woman whose greed ruined a godly man

Delilah (duh-lie-la) was a Philistine woman. The people of her culture worshipped idols, not the God of the Bible. Samson was a Nazarite, which means he had been dedicated to God and set apart to serve God. Samson, much like Jesus many centuries later, was born after an angel visited his mother. His mother could not have children; she was a barren peasant from the tribe of Dan. She is not mentioned by name but is simply referred to as Manoah's wife.

The angel announced to her that she would have a son, but even while she was pregnant, she had to follow strict dietary rules. Her son would also have to follow those rules his whole life and "his head must never be touched by a razor" (Judges 13:5 NIV). He was a blessing to her, a miracle baby. Even his name, Samson, means "little sun." He was born with tremendous strength, created by God to defeat the Philistines. Samson would be an Israelite judge for twenty years.

The Bible says Samson once tore apart a lion with his bare hands. Sadly, however, despite his physical strength, he was morally weak. This was his crippling flaw. Samson had ongoing issues with self-control and lust for women. This poor mindset took him away from God and godly things.

To his parents' dismay, he insisted on marrying a Philistine woman he had fallen in love with. She ended up being killed in their first week of marriage. The Philistines burned her and her father (Judges 15:6 NIV).

Later, the Bible records that he met with a prostitute (Judges 16:1 NIV) and then he met Delilah, another prostitute. He didn't take Delilah into his house as his wife and make a home with her. Instead, they just moved in together, living in sin (having sex outside of marriage). The Philistine leaders heard that they were living together and used Delilah to spy on Samson to learn the secret to his great strength. In all their confrontations and war with the Israelites, they had not been able to beat the power of Samson. They had not been able to defeat him because of his supernatural strength.

Delilah was not only a prostitute living in sin; she also had an issue with money. She loved it. The Philistine leaders who were trying to kill Samson got her involved in their scheme by offering her money for her cooperation in his capture. They promised eleven hundred pieces of silver if she could help them get Samson. This was an obscene amount of money in those times. The cost of silver today is twenty-seven dollars an ounce, which would roughly be a payout of more than $21,000 in biblical times.

She agreed. She was not a follower of the one true God; she worshipped the idol Dagon, like other people of her city. In their society, women did not hold positions in government, nor were they considered leaders. The scheme and attention from the Philistine leaders appealed to her prideful nature as much as her love of money did. *Read 1 Timothy 6:10.*

She lured Samson into her bed. During their "pillow talk" time, she tried to get him to reveal why he was supernaturally strong. He was blinded by his lust and desires and couldn't see through Delilah's lies and her true motives, but he was still a little hesitant to tell his secret.

She tried many times to lure him into telling her the truth about his power but failed. In her last attempt, she used "love" and manipulation. She claimed she just wanted peace between them, and he had to prove he loved her. His guard was down. He told her everything. He shared that his hair had never been cut as part of his Nazarite vow, and that was the source of his power from God. *Read Judges 16:15–20.*

She sent word to the Philistines that she finally knew Samson's secret and to come that night with the money. While he slept, she cut off his hair, and the power of God left him. Just case it hadn't worked, she screamed to wake Samson up, saying, "Samson, the Philistines are upon you!" (Judges 16:20 NIV). He woke up, thinking he would overpower the Philistines as before, but his strength was gone. The Philistines captured Samson but didn't kill him. Rather, they gouged out his eyes, tortured him, and sent him to the city of Gaza to be a common slave, grinding grains. Samson was ruined by lust. After twenty years as a hero of the Israelites, he now lived a life of humiliation.

Read Judges 16:20–22. Delilah didn't seem distraught by what she had done to another human being, never mind her lover. She betrayed his trust. She didn't know God or have a relationship with Him. She was controlled by her selfish desire for position and wealth just as Samson had been controlled by his pride and lust. Once the Philistines had captured Samson, they wanted to throw a festival in celebration of his capture and honor of their pagan god, Dagon. They asked to have Samson come out during the party to humiliate him further. They wanted to exalt

Dagon over Israel's God and show that he was the more powerful god.

Did they forget about the God of Samson and that He was the one true God who will not be mocked? The roof where the party was held had about three thousand people on it. It doesn't say if Delilah was there, but how could they forget her? They brought Samson in and stationed him between two pillars that were holding the roof, not seeing that his hair had begun to grow back. They brought him there to mock him. Samson, felt a stir in his spirit, remembering God's calling on his life. He cried out to the Lord for forgiveness and asked for vengeance on the people who had taken his eyes and tried to elevate their false god above Yahweh. He was born to free and avenge God's people.

Read Judges 16:25–30. At the same time as he was praying, Samson pushed against the pillars, which then collapsed the entire roof. Thousands of people were killed, including the ones who had captured him, probably Delilah, and Samson himself. Paul later wrote (centuries later) a warning about the heart. He said the heart is deceitful, and a deceptive heart (like Delilah's) desires evil things. It is wise not to ignore these words.

After Samson's death, defeat fell on the nation of Israel again. They came under a period of spiritual decline, conquest, and suffering. Solomon later writes about the relationship between Samson and Delilah. He warns men that a deceitful woman may have honey on her lips but getting involved with her will lead to death. Read Ecclesiastes 7:26.

Verses about Delilah:

- ➢ Genesis 34:1–30
- ➢ Joshua 2:1
- ➢ Judges 13:2–5, 24–25; 16:31; 14:5–6; 15:13–16; 16:5, 6, 9–10, 15–20, 28
- ➢ Ecclesiastes 7:26
- ➢ Proverbs 5:3–4; 2:19; 6:27; 23:27
- ➢ Luke 1:26–38
- ➢ 1 Corinthians 10:6

Questions about Delilah:

1. List the outcomes that were achieved through Delilah's actions.
2. What lessons can we learn from the behavior of Delilah?
3. What does the Bible say about the love of money?
4. How can we purify our hearts and our motives?

Fill in the blanks (use the ESV translation):

Judges 6: 9–10: "Now she had men lying in ambush in an inner chamber. And she said to him, 'The _____ are upon you, Samson!' But he snapped the _____, as a thread of flax snaps when it touches the fire. So the _____of his strength was not known. Then Delilah said to Samson, 'Behold, you have _____ me and told me lies. Please tell me how you _____be bound.'"

Personal reflections:

Do you struggle with any form of lust? If yes, how can you surrender that to God?

_____

_____

Write out Matthew 7:6 and reflect on what the passage is saying.

_____

_____

_____

Knowing you are chosen by God to do great things for His glory on earth, how can you better partner with Him and not be ensnared in sin?

_____

_____

What is the danger of sex before marriage according to the Bible?

_____

_____

Naomi

A widow who suffered a great loss but loved others deeply

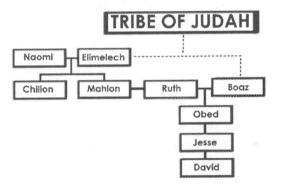

Read Ruth 1:1–6. This is the story of Naomi and her daughters-in-law, Ruth and Orpah. Naomi, her husband, and two sons arrived in Moab, having left their hometown of Bethlehem because of a famine. Her husband died sometime thereafter. Her sons had taken Moabite wives, but neither had been able to have children. She knew children were a blessing from the Lord, so she assumed they were cursed.

Within ten years of losing her husband, both of her sons died—young and prematurely. She fell into a depression and was lonely. Orpah and Ruth stayed with her because they loved Naomi greatly. Naomi heard in Bethlehem that the famine had ended; there was plenty of food and the people were eating well. She decided to leave Moab and make the journey back to Bethlehem and whatever extended family remained. Both Ruth and Orpah decided to go with her.

Shortly after they left on their journey, however, Naomi stopped along the roadside. She had been thinking about these two women who loved her so much. She was thinking they should stay in Moab, their land, and find new husbands. She said to them, "Would you wait for them to grow up and refuse to marry someone else? No, of course not, my daughters! Things are far more bitter for me than for you because the LORD has raised his fist against me" (Ruth 1:13 NLT). She wanted them to find happiness and have children of their own. She was acting selflessly and looking after the future of these young women. She knew in her heart they were devoted to her, but she loved them too and wanted to do what she thought was best for them.

Both women said, no, that they wouldn't leave her, but shortly later, after more urging from Naomi, Orpah changed her mind. She hugged Naomi and turned back to Moab, back to the home of her parents. But according to the Bible, "Ruth replied, 'Don't urge me to leave you or turn back from you. Where you go, I will go. Where you live I will live, and where you die, I will die. Your people will be my people, and your God my God'" (Ruth 4:11 NIV). Naomi had been sharing the true God with these two women who had only been accustomed to idol worship in Moab. Naomi was a great influence on them. Read Deuteronomy 11:26–27.

Ruth said to Naomi that she would go with her no matter the cost. She would serve Naomi's God and be part of her people … abandoning all she had ever known to live in a strange land as a widow. In that culture, cities and lands were strictly divided. Naomi knew it was unlikely that an Israelite would marry a Moabite, and she wanted the best for Ruth. But once Ruth made her declaration of devotion, Naomi knew she was loyal and thanked God for bringing such love into her life after such sorrow and loss.

When they arrived in Bethlehem, Naomi was surprised to be kindly welcomed back into her old city, which she left so many years before; she had changed so much. *Read Ruth 1:20.* She had lost everything. She said to her old friends, "Don't call me Naomi; call me Mara," which means "bitter sorrow." She introduced Ruth, and over time these women came to welcome Ruth because of her devotion to Naomi.

Because they were both widows, Naomi and Ruth needed to find food and a way to support themselves. Ruth went to a wheat farm after the hired harvesters went through. The poor were accustomed to picking up the leftover stalks from the ground for food. This was called "gleaning the field." By Mosaic Law, the farmers had to leave the corners of the field unharvested and weren't allowed to go back a second time to pick up what was missed so that the poor and widows could gather food to eat.

Boaz was an older, wealthy, God-fearing landowner. He was at his field one day observing the harvest with an overseer. He noticed Ruth and asked the overseer who she was. He then told her that she could drink from his well and work on his lands, and he gave orders that no one should bother her. She was grateful and asked why he was so kind to her, an outsider. He replied that he knew of her kindness to her mother-in-law and how she had left her land, parents, and her people to stay with Naomi. He had noticed the great character she displayed and her loving heart toward an older woman who could give her nothing but love.

Boaz had a relationship with God and prayed a special blessing over Ruth. He showed Ruth great kindness during the workday and even gave her additional grain every day to take home to Naomi.

Naomi had a conversation with Ruth about Boaz, and what her future could be with him. Some say she was orchestrating a relationship, but God looks at the heart. Naomi needed to sell her husband's land and needed a male kinsman-redeemer (next of kin) to purchase it.

Naomi told Ruth to wash, put on her best clothes, and go down to the threshing floor where they processed the grain. After Boaz was asleep, Ruth was to lie down by his feet, which in those days were considered the most vulnerable part of the body. When Boaz awoke in the middle of the night, he saw her asleep there and woke her up. They started talking and she told him he was their close relative. In this culture, the closest male relative would marry a widow and tend to the land that had belonged to her husband so she could have a child in the name of the deceased husband. The child would be raised to carry on the family name of the deceased. Naomi knew this was a great opportunity for Ruth to find love and live a full life. In obedience, Ruth spoke with Boaz and asked if he would fulfill that role of a kinsman-redeemer.

Boaz, however, said he was *not* the closest relative, but if that man didn't want to assume the role of the kinsman-redeemer, Boaz would. He was saying, "If he won't marry you and care for you, I will," because he knew she was a godly woman.

Boaz wasted no time the next morning. He gathered ten elders of the city to be witnesses. Then Boaz invited that closest relative to come to the meeting. He explained that

Naomi was going to sell the land that had belonged to her husband and, as the law required, the closest male relative had the first option to purchase it. The man initially said yes, he would buy the land. Boaz explained that if he did, he would have to take care of Naomi and marry Ruth. If they had a son, that son would inherit the property, not his current children.

After careful consideration, the man decided not to buy the land as he already had a wife and children and didn't want the conflict that would arise. Therefore, Boaz was free to marry Ruth and buy the land. The man who decided not to take the land gave Boaz his sandal, which according to their culture symbolized a binding contract and rights to the land and to marry Ruth.

Boaz married Ruth and took in Naomi. They had a son, Obed, whom Naomi considered her grandchild. Boaz was noted as a nobleman. Ruth was rewarded for her faithfulness. Obed became the grandfather of King David. It was from this bloodline that Jesus would come. Interestingly, Boaz's mother was Rahab, the prostitute from Jericho. She too is listed in the lineage of Christ. With God, *no one is overlooked*; everyone has a place in God's kingdom. *Read 1 Peter 5:10.*

Verses about Naomi:

> Genesis 19:36–37
> Deuteronomy 7:3–4; 11:26–28; 23:3–4; 28:18
> Ruth 1:10,15–22; 3:1; 4:14, 18
> Jeremiah 48:1–47

Questions about Naomi:

1. Can you name a blessing in Naomi's early life?
2. Was she a good mother-in-law and why?
3. Why did she rename herself?
4. Do you see a redemption story through her life?

Fill in the blanks (use the ESV translation):

Ruth 1: 16–18. "But Ruth said, 'Do not _____ me to leave you or to return from following you. For where _____ I will go, and where you _____ I will lodge. Your people shall be my people, and your _____. Where you die I will die, and there will I be buried. May the _____ do so to me and more also if anything but death parts me from you.' And when Naomi _____ that she was determined to go with her, she said, '_____.'"

Personal reflections:

Where do you see God most in Naomi's story?

_____

_____

If God asked you to do something, even if it meant going alone, how would you respond?

_____

_____

What does the Bible say about sorrow?

_____

_____

Write 2 Corinthians 5:17 and how it applies to Naomi, then how it applies to you.

_____

_____

_____

Zipporah

A woman who was a steadfast, honorable wife to a great leader

Zipporah (zuh-pore-uh) was Moses's wife. She was the oldest daughter of Jethro, a priest of Midian and descendant of Abraham through his wife Keturah (whom he married after Sarah died, Genesis 25:1–2). Her name means "bird," maybe sparrow. We see her story unfold in Exodus 2:16–21.

Moses, who was raised in the palace as an Egyptian, the adopted son of Pharaoh's daughter, ends up killing a guard who was whipping a Jew, one of "his people." Out of fear for his life when his crime is discovered, he flees Egypt and ends up in the wilderness. *Read Exodus 2:16–17.*

While he was around Midian, he needed water. As he approached a well, he saw several women being bullied for the water they had just drawn for their sheep. Moses stepped in and defended them. When they saw Moses, they thought he was Egyptian. The girls' father, Jethro, was impressed that Moses had helped his daughters get their water, and he invited him to dinner. Jethro later gave Zipporah to Moses as his wife.

Read Numbers 12:1. Later, the Bible tells us that Moses's sister, Miriam, and brother, Aaron, had issues with him because he had "married a Cushite." The Jewish text and Bible give context to Zipporah's culture and beauty. Cush typically meant Ethiopian, but when she married Moses, God calls them Israelites. Their union makes them his royal bloodline. God doesn't make a distinction between races here. We see Miriam having a big issue with Moses's wife because of her race. This leads to God allowing leprosy to fall upon Miriam for her sin of speaking against Moses and his wife.

Zipporah was married to Moses at least forty years (during his time as a shepherd in the wilderness), possibly longer, before she died. As a descendant of Abraham herself, she likely knew the law of God about circumcision of a newborn, but for some reason, Moses had not circumcised their firstborn son, Gershom—a big risk and disobedience to God. Genesis 17:12 shows us the law of circumcision, outlining that it should take place eight days after birth. Moses did not do that with their son.

In Exodus 4:24-27 NIV, Moses heads back to Egypt with his family, as God had commanded him at the burning bush. But on their way, the Bible says, "The Lord met Moses and was about to kill him." We see Zipporah grab a flint knife and circumcise Gershom before God can kill Moses for his disobedience.

We don't know why Moses had not done it, but God was patient with him for a long time. This shows us that when God uses a person for His plan, He is very patient to a point. But eventually, judgment will come. Moses's life was saved by Zipporah's action. She stepped in with her obedience and knowledge of the law and fear of the Lord. We see this many times in the word: someone's obedience saves another. God doesn't want to punish us, so He often waits until the last possible moment to execute judgment—like the story of Noah and the flood. God is always calling us into repentance because He is merciful and wants to bless us.

God had chosen Moses as His voice on Earth, and He needed to purge him of sin—disobedience in this case—so he could be used righteously. Before God uses us in big ways, He needs to deal with any hidden sin that can be used as a legal right by Satan to stall God's plan. God wanted to establish Moses as a mighty figure of His power. God dealt with him, and deals with us—sometimes severely—to accomplish His will. We see in the word how He dealt with His prophets in private before they were released for ministry. Moses needed to repent before going to Pharaoh, and he did.

We know that Moses wasn't a great public speaker. He stuttered and his brother, Aaron, often spoke for him. Moses didn't start out great; he was spoiled and prideful and had serious anger issues. We see this when he murdered that Egyptian and left him in the desert. The Bible says that at the end of his life, he was the meekest, humblest man on earth. In the process of following God's heart, we are sanctified in His image. *Read Numbers 12:3.*

Zipporah was a good wife, noted twice in the word as beautiful. She was given to Moses by God for her qualities, knowing that Moses needed her obedience and grace. As wives, we have great influence over our husbands. "Praise the Lord, all you nations. Praise Him, all you people of the Earth. For He loves us with unfailing love, and the Lord's faithfulness endures forever. Praise the Lord" (Psalm 117:12 NIV).

Verses about Zipporah:

➢ Genesis 17:12
➢ Exodus 2:16–21; 4:22; 24:24–27
➢ Numbers 10:29; 12:1,13
➢ Judges 4:11
➢ Psalm 117
➢ Jeremiah 13:23
➢ Amos 9:7

Questions about Zipporah:

1. When reading the story of Zipporah, what stood out the most to you?
2. What about her grabbing the flint knife felt like a divine intervention?
3. What is God saying about being a godly wife through the story of Zipporah?

Fill in the blanks (use the ESV translation):

Exodus 4:24–26: "At a lodging place on the way the _____met him and sought to put him to _____. Then Zipporah took a _____and cut off her son's foreskin and touched Moses' feet with it and said, 'Surely you are a _____ of blood to me!' So he let him alone. It was then that she said, 'A bridegroom of blood,' because of the _____.'"

Personal reflections:

Would you have responded the same as Zipporah in the same situation?

_____

When someone sins in your life do you bring it to their attention in the hope that they will repent?

_____

Write out Proverbs 27:17 and what this means to you.

_____

_____

Why was Zipporah an example of a God-fearing, honorable wife?

_____

_____

_____

Ruth

A woman who displayed godly purity inside and out

Family Tree of Ruth

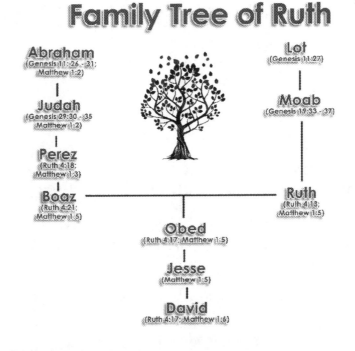

Abraham
(Genesis 11:26 - 31;
Matthew 1:2)

|

Judah
(Genesis 29:30 - 35
Matthew 1:2)

|

Perez
(Ruth 4:18;
Matthew 1:3)

|

Boaz
(Ruth 4:21;
Matthew 1:5)

Lot
(Genesis 11:27)

|

Moab
(Genesis 19:33 - 37)

|

Ruth
(Ruth 4:13;
Matthew 1:5)

Obed
(Ruth 4:17; Matthew 1:5)

|

Jesse
(Matthew 1:5)

|

David
(Ruth 4:17; Matthew 1:6)

We know from the story in the book of Ruth how the dynamic was between Naomi, Orpah, and Ruth. We know Ruth was a childless young widow in Moab. We know how scripture explains her heart. When Naomi decided to leave Moab and return to Israel, Ruth determined to go with her. She and Naomi arrived in the land of Bethlehem at the time of the harvest season, and she immediately went to Boaz's land to glean grain and provide food for herself and Naomi. We can see God working in these circumstances and drawing them together. Naomi had to ask God when He was opening and closing doors and allow space for the Holy Spirit to work. She knew the obedience of Isaac, Jacob, and the miracle of Sarah, and knew God partners with us for miracles.

When Ruth's eyes met Boaz's in his field while she was gleaning grain, she asked him why she had found his favor. He told her it was because of her loving heart for her mother-in-law and courage to start over in a foreign land. This shows us insight into her character and heart posture: courage, great gratitude, and loyalty. Ruth was permitted to continue to glean in his fields and even get water from his water jars and sit with his servants. He told her that she could have what she needed. Boaz had a good heart.

We learn later he intended to marry her, if her closest relative did not. In this union, he would also inherit the responsibility of caring for an aging Naomi as well. Boaz did many things to include Ruth in their culture customs. When they would break to eat, Ruth, knowing her place, would stay with the reapers, but Boaz invited her to share his bread and dip it in the wine vinegar. It was not the custom to invite women to eat, especially foreign women. Perhaps the fact that his mother had not been an Israelite gave him compassion for a foreigner trying to fit in.

Ruth knew there was something different about the heart of Boaz. She had a humble heart, too, which allowed God to work with their loss and loneliness for good. It is the nature of God to divinely intervene and bring blessings to those who love and honor Him. Ruth became known in her town as a woman who cared for people, genuine and loyal. Ruth possessed a spirit of inspiration and concern for others.

Weeks passed as Ruth kept gleaning in the fields and building a friendship with Boaz. Naomi told her that once the harvest was over and Boaz was sleeping on the threshing floor to keep guard over his harvest, she was to sneak in and lay down by his feet. He would awaken, see her act of humility in asking for his protection, and have kindness on her and take her as his wife as her "kinsman-redeemer." Ruth was probably shocked, not accustomed to this Israelite way of doing things, but she wanted to please Naomi and trusted her. Moses had created a long-standing law for a widow. To keep a widow's deceased husband's name relevant, the husband's brother or next of kin would marry the widow. The firstborn son out of that marriage would carry on the deceased's family name.

As far as Naomi knew, that was Boaz; but in fact, it wasn't. Boaz, therefore, had to offer the marriage and land to the kinsman who *was* the rightful heir. But after realizing that his children would not be able to inherit the property, that relative declined. This gave Boaz the legal standing under Moses's law to marry and purchase the land of Naomi's late husband. According to custom, he met with ten elders of his city to discuss the matter, and it was agreed Boaz could marry Ruth.

God moved and showed us which of the two men He intended Ruth to marry. When Boaz married Ruth, he didn't forget Naomi, who came to live with them too. Ruth gave birth to a son whom she named Obed, who was in the chosen lineage of Christ, the Messiah. She became a mother in the line of the Redeemer. The Bible has only two books named after women, Ruth and Esther. To this day, these women are much respected.

Ruth displayed great courage and honor to her family and people who were close to her. God used her to show us great lessons of humility, compassion, and purity in women. It also shows us how much God looks at the heart.

Ruth's story still influences people today. This woman with three strikes against her—poor, childless widow, and a foreigner—still loved God and her fellow man. She experienced God's favor. Her son, Obed, who was King David's grandfather, was chosen by God to become a forefather in the lineage of Jesus the Messiah. God once again protected this bloodline. Ruth's influence is far-reaching and wasn't just restricted to the Hebrew land and people. She is also one of the five women in the genealogy of Christ alongside Tamar, Rahab (Boaz's mother), Bathsheba, and Mary.

Verses about Ruth:

> Genesis 2:18; 24:6–7; 29:30
> Leviticus 19:9–10
> Deuteronomy 25:5–10
> Ruth 3:5, 9, 15; 4:1–10; 1:16; 2:4, 8–14, 19–20; 3:2–4
> Matthew 1:5

Questions about Ruth:

1. Why did Ruth decide to go with Naomi?
2. What do you think God favored in Ruth?
3. List some of Ruth's good qualities.
4. What about Ruth and Boaz's courtship and marriage do you admire?

Fill in the blanks (use the ESV translation):

Ruth 1:8–10. "But Naomi said to her two daughters-in-law, 'Go, _____ each of you to her _____ house. May the LORD deal kindly with you, as you have dealt with the dead and with me. The LORD grant that you may find rest, each of you in the house of a husband!' Then she _____ them, and they lifted up their voices and _____.

And they said to her, '_____, we will return with you to _____ people.'"

Personal reflections:

Do you possess a heart and concern for others? If not, then why and how can you change this?

_____

_____

Write out Proverbs 3:3 and how you can reflect this passage in your own life.

_____

_____

Look up the meaning of your name and find a scripture you can use as your flagship verse for yourself.

_____

Ruth respected her elders in every situation she was presented in. Do you do the same in your own life with your parents, spouse, and boss? If not, how can you better follow the Bible's example of obedience to authority?

_____

_____

Week Four Review

Review your Bible verses for each woman. Pray over new revelation through the word.

Weekly Challenge:

Ask God to help you demonstrate humility to others. Let God know you are willing to be used by Him for His glory in even the smallest way.

Prayer:

Heavenly Father, I come before Your throne of grace wanting to be a great instrument for Your kingdom. I know how important it is for You to have all our trust and to come to You with humility. Lord, as I learn to humble myself, can You help me in the areas that still challenge me? Lord, search my heart for any evil and lust of the flesh or idolatry in it and remove the root. I want to serve You only. Lord, You come first for me in my affections, priorities, and time. You have done so many great things in my life, and I will continue to look through the filter of Your majesty and know that You will not fail me. I want my life to honor You. Help me identify sin areas in my life. I ask the Holy Spirit to continue to help mold me in the image of Christ each day. Thank you, Lord, I love You, amen.

Weekly Declaration:

I declare I will not just survive but thrive. I will prosper in every situation that is presented to me. I will not give up on the passions and dreams that God has placed inside my heart. I will not look at God's delays as His denials and remember to submit to His perfect timing. This is my declaration.

WOW Week Five

Prayer: Lord, I invite You into this space to be seated in the highest place of honor. I exalt You and desire to learn Your ways. Help me learn Your word and let it take deep root in my life. Let me learn all You want for me today. Open my heart, eyes, and ears to Your teaching. Let me be changed by it today. In Jesus's name, amen.

This week will study the lives of Jephthah's daughter, Elizabeth, and Bathsheba.

Jephthah's Daughter

A woman who paid the price for a foolish vow

Jephthah's story plays out in the book of Judges. His land was in the northeast part of Syria called Tob, next to the Sea of Galilee. Jephthah was a skilled warrior alongside the greats like Gideon. He was faithful and loved the Lord very much. He did not start in life with very much. His mother was a prostitute and his father had other children who wanted to cut him out of the inheritance. He fled after his half brothers and sisters refused to give him part of their father's inheritance. *Read Judges 11:1–3.*

A war broke out, however, and the people needed Jephthah's expertise to fight them. His half brothers, who had once rejected him, asked him to be their army's commander. He was hesitant. *Read Judges 11:7–9.*

Jephthah pleaded with the Lord for victory. He made a vow to God that he would offer a burnt sacrifice of the first thing he saw when he arrived home if God would give him the battle victory. The Israelites won the battle. *Read Judges 11:31.*

Upon his return, his only daughter, who is not named in scripture (she is only known to us as Jephthah's daughter), was excited to see her father when he got back from battle. As Jephthah was entering his gate to his home, his daughter ran out to greet him. *Read Judges 11:35.*

Distraught and saddened, he believed that he must sacrifice her to God. In the land at this time, the people had strayed from following God's laws completely. The thought of human sacrifice was more acceptable than breaking a vow, especially because the surrounding nations frequently practiced human sacrifice. Human sacrifice is always against God's laws, but the laws had been adulterated, watered down by foreign morality.

In modern churches today, we see that we have allowed the culture of our times and our world to infiltrate the church and our homes with movies, music, clothing, and sermons that do not agree with God's desires, according to the Bible.

Jephthah's daughter told her father that she understood the vow he had made to God and was willing to be his sacrifice. She did request to go into the mountains with her female friends for two months to mourn the fact she would die a virgin and never have children. This was an additional pathos of her fate, a second consequence—to never marry. Some scholars think Jephthah gave her to the church, the priesthood, for the remainder of her life. However, in this theory, that would still be an honor. He could still see her and she would still be alive, serving God. But there is no joy in the scriptures, only sadness. We can assume that he did give her as a burnt offering to God. *Read Judges 11:39–40.*

After this was finished, the innocent daughter became a symbol of obedience and tragedy, and the Israelite women went out to honor Jephthah's daughter every year for four days. This wrong sacrifice opened the door for sin and a curse to come over the people later in the book of Judges. Jephthah's daughter was young, innocent, and unmarried. She was loyal to her father and served the Lord.

At the time, however, it was her father's legal right to do to her as he pleased. The people had allowed the influence of other cultures in the land to shape what they believed was true, which was not the biblical way to worship the Lord. Other gods demanded flesh, blood, and human sacrifices, but the Lord called these detestable acts. Somehow, these supposed God-fearing people had started to practice the wicked acts of the surrounding peoples.

Jephthah's daughter's story shows us not to make unwise vows to God that make no sense but bind you to your word. Sometimes we pray things like, "Let my daughter live and I'll never sin again!" These vows are silly and hard or impossible to keep as sinful people. Bargaining with the Lord has been seen in scripture, and in the right context with pure-heart motives, we can see the Lord occasionally honors them. But avoiding silly vows is the big lesson in this story. It cost Jephthah his only child and caused many other consequences.

Verses about Jephthah's daughter:

> ➤ Judges 11
> ➤ Proverbs 18:21

Questions about Jephthah's daughter:

1. Why is human sacrifice against the Lord's will?
2. Why do you believe Jephthah's daughter did not protest the vow?
3. What is your big takeaway from this story?

Fill in the blanks (use the ESV translation):

Judges 11:30–31. "And Jephthah made a _____ to the LORD, and said, 'If thou wilt give the Ammonites into my hand, then _____ comes forth from the _____ of my house to meet me when I return victorious from the Ammonites, shall be the LORD's, and I will _____ him up for a _____ offering.'"

Judges 11:35. "And when he saw her, he _____ his clothes, and said, 'Alas, my daughter! you have brought me very low, and you have become the cause of _____ to me; for I have opened my _____ to the LORD, and I cannot take back my _____.'"

Personal reflections:

Why does God take our words so seriously, especially vows?

_____

_____

What vows have I made to God?

_____

_____

Write out Proverbs 18:21 and give an example in your life for both.

_____

_____

Why does God wants our obedience over a sacrifice?

_____

Elizabeth

A woman whose heart was pure, chosen by God to be the mother of the one before Christ

The story of Elizabeth is found in the gospel of Luke 1. Her name means "my God is a faithful God." She was the barren mother of John the Baptist. She was married to Zechariah, who was a priest. She was a descendant of Aaron, Moses's brother.

The Bible offers us a lens to see into biblical times. The worst curse any Jewish woman could suffer at the time was to be barren. A husband could divorce his wife if she were barren. It was a severe thing to endure. *Read Luke 1:11–17.* We need to learn the Bible and understand the context and culture to understand the scripture. Luke is the author of this gospel and writes in great detail and in chronological order. He was a physician with great compassion for people. More women are mentioned in his gospel than any other. God was raising the position of women to be one of honor.

When Zechariah was told he was going to have a son, he did not believe it. Even though he was a priest, he lacked faith. Because of this lack of faith, God silenced him until the promise was fulfilled. God disciplined Zechariah and struck him dumb. In the meantime, Elizabeth doesn't move in her standing of faith in her promise of a son. She allowed God to speak to her husband and chastise him without weighing in on the process. *Read Luke 1:19–20.*

It is very similar to the Abraham and Sarah story but in reverse. It is the man that does not believe. Age is not a factor in God's ability. Elizabeth understood the power of prayer and expected God to answer her prayers. She knew God heard her and He was listening. Luke 1:36 tells us that Mary is pregnant, and the scripture tells us that Elizabeth is pregnant also—at the same time, but a few months further along. For with God, nothing shall be impossible.

Read Luke 1:35–36. God was going to do the impossible on earth. The Bible says He is no respecter of persons. Elizabeth and Mary were good friends, but also cousins. Elizabeth was Mary's mentor. Elizabeth prayed for her womb and sought the Lord to change her circumstance. She became pregnant with a son who would be known as John the Baptist.

Her cousin Mary also became pregnant with Jesus shortly after. When Mary came to visit Elizabeth and walked up to her, the Bible says John leaped in Elizabeth's womb for joy. Mary turned to Elizabeth during this time in her pregnancy and stayed with her for three months. It was spent together in friendship, fellowship, and great discussions about God, purpose, and their babies. After all, these were the two most important babies to ever live. John the Baptist was destined to be the forerunner to Christ, and Jesus, the Messiah, would be the savior to all humanity.

God had a plan to redeem all of humanity because of His great love for us. He sent His own son in the form of a baby to grow, teach, transform hearts, and eventually die for our sins. Elizabeth was the first woman to confess that Jesus was Lord and Savior when He was still in the womb. She taught her son that he must become less—decrease—so Jesus could be greater (increase). John later lost his life for Jesus.

Small groups and mentorship are important to God. God knows that mentors help to shape, push, and walk with you during your faith journey. Young women need godly wisdom and mentorship from older or mature Christians. At this point in history, God had been silent for four hundred years (from the end of the Old Testament prophets) until now. Elizabeth was a light in a dark world. She loved the Lord and had a great marriage—equally yoked. She walked in God's commandments and the Bible calls her "blameless." She wasn't without sin; she was human and imperfect, but she was "blameless." She lived beyond reproach; she avoided anything evil, anything that would compromise her faith. Her appearance, choices, her words were without evil. She presented as a follower of Christ.

Elizabeth was never jealous of Mary for being picked to carry the Messiah, even though she was older, wiser, and more experienced in life. She decided to trust God and His way, knowing God's ways were higher than her own. She did not waver or hesitate. Verse 25 says God looked on her with compassion and opened her womb to have John the Baptist after being barren for many years. She gave God all the glory. She said God had taken away her reproach. Read Luke 1:45.

Verses about Elizabeth:

- ➤ Luke 1; 1:45
- ➤ Hebrews 12:5–6

Questions about Elizabeth:

1. Why do you think God chose Elizabeth to be the mother of John the Baptist?
2. Why do you think God chastened Zechariah?
3. What is something from the story of Elizabeth you can apply to your own life?

Fill in the blanks (use the ESV translation):

Luke 1:41–42. "And when Elizabeth heard the greeting of Mary, the baby _____ in her womb. And Elizabeth was _____ with the _____, and she exclaimed with a loud cry, 'Blessed are you among women, and blessed is the _____ of your womb!'"

Matthew 11:11. "Truly, I say to you, among those _____ of women there has arisen no one _____ than John the Baptist. Yet the one who is _____ in the kingdom of heaven is _____ than he."

Personal reflections

What have I learned during the Lord's chastening of my life?

_____

Why does the Bible say God is the only giver and taker of life?

_____

Do I aspire to be blameless in my love journey with Jesus?

_____

Who was John the Baptist in your own words?

_____

Write out Hebrews 12:5–6 and reflect on God's love for us.

_____

_____

_____

Bathsheba

A woman caught in the crosshairs of the lust of a king

David had already been a great king of Israel for seven and a half years before he encountered Bathsheba. David was a righteous king and highly respected in all the land of Israel.

It had been many years since David had been in a battle to fight on the frontlines seeking God's will over the land. Now he was staying in the palace, shrinking back from responsibility, sitting in his comfort zone. Because of these many years of inactivity as the king, he became ensnared in Satan's plan of temptation.

While on his palace terrace, he saw Bathsheba bathing on the rooftop of her home, and he began to desire her lustfully. David was an overcomer of many things but was disobedient in one major area of his life: women. He desired Bathsheba and sent for her. His thoughts determined his actions. The Bible gives us great instruction on keeping our thoughts in line with godly things because doing otherwise leads to sin—much like King David's example.

By order of the royal court, David summoned Bathsheba to come to dinner that very night. The Bible says that she was unusually beautiful. Her father was a war hero. Her husband, Uriah, was away fighting battles. Despite David knowing that she was married, he slept with her. A couple of months later Bathsheba sent word to David that she was pregnant.

Bathsheba was not the instigator of the events that occurred; however, the Bible does not say she is completely blameless either. Although we must ask ourselves if she could have refused the king, we don't know. Perhaps Bathsheba could have resisted David, and talked some sense into him and explained to him the consequences of the affair before it happened. But she did not. To cover up her pregnancy and the affair, David came up with a plan. He was nervous that his sin of adultery would be found out, so he called for Uriah to come home. He hatched a plan to encourage Uriah to go home for the night to sleep with his wife and rest. However, Uriah refused to sleep with his wife while his fellow soldiers were off fighting.

David's plan failed, and he was filled with anger and fear that his actions would be discovered. When Uriah went back to war, King David sent a note to the army commander with instructions to have Uriah put at the front of the fighting and then to withdraw support so that Uriah would be killed. When Bathsheba found out Uriah had died, she mourned him. When the time of mourning was over, she was brought to King David to be his new wife (2 Samuel 11:27 NIV).

Read Deuteronomy 28:1–6. God needed to correct this and called David to repentance for what he had done. The Bible is very clear that what David did displeased the Lord (2 Samuel 11:27 NIV). God sent the prophet Nathan to visit King David, who in a unique way confronted him about his sin and made clear the Lord's disapproval and displeasure. David cried out to God in his shame for months, writing some of the most powerful lamenting psalms of the

Bible: "Oh God, Oh God, How I search for You …" (Psalm 63:1 NIV). Even though David did repent for his sin, Nathan told David that the son Bathsheba was expecting would die. God clearly explains there are consequences to our sin. While He will forgive us, the Bible never covers up sin. Instead the Bible exposes it so Jesus can redeem us from it.

God had called young David as a shepherd boy for a great destiny, and he needed to be chastened by the Lord for this horrific sin. God the Father will correct and chasten us so that the discipline shapes our character to be more like Christ. Even though Christ had not been born yet in David's time, it was still God's plan to bring David back into alignment with the will of the Father. He used an earthly man, Nathan, to bring this message. According to the law of Moses, both David and Bathsheba deserved to die, but God was gracious towards them. David needed to confess and repent, which he did. His life was spared, but his child would die.

Read Leviticus 20:10. There was a double curse on David's life because in addition to the adulterous action with Bathsheba, he had ordered the murder of Uriah. God punished him for this sin of murder. God told him that the sword would never depart from his house again (2 Samuel 12:10 NIV). As part of that consequence, David's concubines were dishonored by one of his sons, Absalom, in the eyes of Israel. He pitched a tent and slept with his fathers' concubines in front of Israel for all to see. He later tried to overthrow his father and sought to kill him. David's three oldest sons, Amnon, Absalom, and Adonijah, all died very violent deaths.

Although the Bible shares the stories of disobedience, it also shares the heart of God and His grace. David writes in Psalms about the freedom of forgiveness. We can learn a lot from this relationship with him and Bathsheba and what this sin did to transform a king's heart.

The Bible never mentions Bathsheba's feelings, although we can assume that she did feel guilty for the aftermath of their affair and the death of her husband and firstborn son. But because Bathsheba was able to repent and confess the sin, and endure the reality and consequences of that sin, God bestowed grace on her.

The next son that David and Bathsheba had was named Solomon. Solomon would later become the wisest and richest king on earth. Bathsheba would raise her son to know God and become an important intermediary person in his life and public office affairs. A good intermediary is a person who acts as a link between two people to bring about agreement and reconciliation. In the Bible, this is Jesus, who stood in the gap for all of humanity and took upon Himself the curse of our sin and now intercedes for us. *Read 1 Timothy 2:5.*

The story of Bathsheba and David is relatable today. It shows the mercy and goodness of God. Once you repent and surrender in your heart, God can and will restore you to greatness and blessing. Bathsheba's example shows us that women in the church, and life, cannot play the harlot. They need to hold to a standard of modesty, virtue, and righteousness. It is essential to not be a stumbling block, a temptress for other men. It is so easy to have something that was intended as a blessing become a curse. *Read James 4:17.*

Bathsheba did not start as a positive influence. However, once she surrendered and allowed God to move in her heart, she become a godly, gracious, and wonderful example of a woman after God's heart.

Verses about Bathsheba:

➢ Genesis 3:6; 39:9
➢ Leviticus 20:10
➢ 1 Samuel 25: 23–31; 30:1–6
➢ 2 Samuel 11:1, 27; 12:1–10,14,19; 13:28–30; 18:3–4, 14; 16:22
➢ 1 Kings 15:5; 2:24–25
➢ Job 31:1
➢ Psalm 32:1–2, 51; 63:1
➢ Matthew 1:6
➢ 2 Timothy 1:7
➢ James 1:14–15; 4:17

Questions about Bathsheba:

1. What could Bathsheba have done to prevent the demise of David?
2. List some of the consequences of David and Bathsheba's sin.
3. What can we learn from Bathsheba today?
4. What is the greatest warning of this story that God wants us to learn?
5. What does repentance do for us and why does the Bible require us to repent for sin?

Fill in the blanks (use the ESV translation):

2 Samuel 12:9–10. "Why have you _____ the word of the LORD, to do what is evil in his sight? You have _____ down _____ the Hittite with the sword and have taken _____ to be your wife and have killed him with the sword of the Ammonites. Now therefore the _____ shall never depart from your house, because you have despised me and have taken the wife of Uriah the Hittite to be your wife."

Personal reflections:

Write out Job 31:1.

_____

_____

_____

How can I be more modest?

_____

Am I affected by the lusts of the eyes?

_____

Write Philippians 4:8 and give an example for each, prayer, petition and thanksgiving.

_____

_____

_____

Week Five Review

Review your Bible verses for each woman. Pray over new revelation through the word.

Weekly Challenge:

Ask God to help you take the leading of the Holy Spirit, to humble yourself to His will. Ask God to help you take steps that align with His timing and not ours.

Prayer:

Heavenly Father, I come before Your throne of grace asking to be forgiven for my sins against You. Lord, I am sorry for the times I did not trust You, obey You, or when I become a stumbling block to others. I desire to be pure and righteous before You. Lord, help me hate sin, hate my sin because of what it cost Christ on the cross. May I not forget Your blood that was shed for me. I pray that it equips me to stand in Your truth and abide inside Your will for my life. I want to be where You need me to be, I want to go where You need me to go, and I will be obedient. Father, search my heart and uproot anything evil, self-serving, not pleasing to You. Lord, rip the root right out and fill my heart with Your love, peace, and truth. I do not want to be someone who digs in her heels, God, but rather someone who immediately surrenders to You. Help me remain inside Your will. Let Your voice be the loudest. Let Your truth and laws govern my heart and my lips so I speak life over things. In Jesus's mighty name I pray this with my whole heart's conviction, amen.

Weekly Declaration:

I declare that I am a people builder. I will look for opportunities where I can build people up, affirming them. I will let others know they are valued and loved. I will call forth the seeds of greatness in other people. This is my declaration.

WOW Week Six

Prayer: Lord, I trust You with my time. Allow the voice of the Holy Spirit to teach me Your ways and convict my heart of any hidden sin so I am not separated from You. I ask that You come into this space and fill this room with Your loving presence. I trust Your nature and Your unfailing love for me. Help me to learn Your Word and truth so it never departs from my heart. I love You, kind Jesus. In Your holy name, amen.

This week we will study the lives of Jezebel, Huldah, Lydia, and Salome.

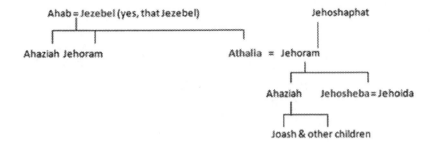

Jezebel

A woman who went after God's anointed and failed

Read 1 Kings 18:1–6. This tells the story of the weak, wicked King Ahab and his manipulative queen wife, Jezebel. Jezebel was a princess before she married and became a queen. They worshipped Baal and other idols. Her biggest mistake was thinking the God of Israel, the one true God, was equal to the god of Baal, which she worshipped. She thought Yahweh was a local god who cared for the Israelites only.

King Ahab was an insecure, wicked king who coveted the vineyard beside the palace. He offered the owner of the vineyard, Naboth, whatever sum of money he wanted because the vineyard was fruitful and beautiful. Naboth refused to sell it as it was his inheritance and had been in his family for years.

Naboth's land was his legacy and business. It was a beautiful plantation full of gorgeous fields and gardens, and King Ahab wanted it for himself. When Naboth rejected King Ahab's offer, Ahab pouted like a little boy. Back home in the palace, he was so beside himself, he refused to eat. Jezebel asked him why he was upset. He told her the story and her reply revealed the depth of her prideful, evil heart.

She stated that Ahab was king, and he deserved the land. So she devised a plot. Jezebel wrote letters to the elders of the city under King Ahab's name and using the king's seal. The letters instructed the elders to have a feast. There they would declare that Naboth had "cursed" God and the king and they would stone him to death.

The elders did as instructed. They threw a big party and planted two men as false witnesses there to discredit Naboth, saying he had cursed God and the king. They smeared Naboth's good character and violated God's ninth commandment. It worked. The courts believed these two liars and Naboth was sentenced to death by stoning. *Read Deuteronomy 19:15.*

Jezebel and Ahab were already in violation of the first commandment, "You shall not have any gods before me." Now they had also broken the ninth commandment: "You shall not bear false witness against your neighbor," and even the tenth, which states, "You shall not covet anything that belongs to your neighbor." God was upset by this, so He sent Elijah, who was a whistleblower, a truth-teller, and a prophet.

Jezebel was a false prophetess, a false teacher of truth, a teacher of lies. She persecuted the real prophets of God and had ordered their deaths. She was used by Satan as a real instrument of destruction. Because Jezebel and Ahab were both narcissists, no one was allowed to say no to them.

Ahab and Jezebel were by far the most wicked and evil people in the Bible, a modern-day Bonnie and Clyde. They committed horrific crimes in the name of Baal. They worshipped their fertility gods and prosperity gods and opened the door to witchcraft. Once Jezebel found out that Naboth had died, she urged Ahab to go over and take possession of the vineyard they had "won."

Sometime later, there was a three-year drought in the land, and Jezebel was on a rampage killing prophets of God. Obadiah was the master of the house for the king, and he feared—obeyed—the Lord, even though his king and queen worshipped pagan idols. Obadiah heard Jezebel was slaughtering prophets, so he hid fifty in one cave and fifty in another to spare them from her wrath. He cared for them and fed them. During his journey back from the caves, Obadiah encountered Elijah. *Read 1 Kings 18:7–13.*

Obadiah was fearful when meeting Elijah because he knew Ahab was on the hunt for him, blaming Elijah for the drought. But God had sent Elijah to warn King Ahab and Queen Jezebel of the punishment coming to them and to set up a little competition.

Read 1 Kings 18:14–22. When Ahab met Elijah, he said, "Oh, here comes trouble." Back in that culture, much like today, prophets were unwelcome truth tellers and scapegoats, and were considered trouble. Elijah fired back and said, "Well, actually, *you* are the one causing trouble, getting God's people to worship Baal and introducing witchcraft." Ahab had introduced a counterfeit to God's righteousness and justice needed to be done. Like Nathan, Elijah called out his king for murder, in this case the murder of Naboth for his vineyard. Just like God dealt with David and his son, he must deal with Ahab.

Elijah said it was time for the people to stop wavering between Jezebel's false gods and the one true God. So he set up a contest between God and her god Baal and assembled the four hundred and fifty "priests" of Baal, to match one lone servant of God, Elijah, on Mt. Carmel.

So the battle was set; the winner takes all. Altars were set up with a sacrifice prepared. Whichever god brought down fire to consume the sacrifice would be the one that would be worshipped. The god that answered by fire would be acknowledged as the real god. Elijah was a true prophet of God and went to Mt. Carmel to essentially settle a bet. Jezebel had assembled her priests of Baal at an altar where they had often sacrificed animals, then lit their fire to consume the sacrifice. But this would be different. This was a showdown because Baal was supposed to be the god of storms, lightning, and power, and they were expecting this to be the biggest display of fire and power from their idol god. This, in their minds, should have been an open-and-shut "win" for them. But we know that Baal is not the true god and has no power.

So that morning the priests of Baal built a huge altar with bull offerings. They started to sing and dance for Baal and worship him, asking him to bring down fire and triumph as the one true god. Hours went by and nothing happened … crickets. Absolute silence from Baal.

By evening, the people were tired of waiting, and the prophets were annoyed and exhausted. So they resorted to cutting themselves on their arms and legs and letting the blood gush out. This, I believe, was the result of the demonic forces happening when they opened a door to the worship of idols and witchcraft. Anyone who has "seen" a demon by vision, hallucination, or in a dream knows they are cut up and tattooed from head to toe.

Meanwhile, Elijah was an onlooker from the other altar. He started mocking them and teasing them about the lack of power and presence from their god. It was embarrassing for them. Elijah was saying things to them like, "Where is your god…? Maybe he's on a trip." They were tired, frustrated, and humiliated and eventually they gave up.

Elijah then took center stage. It was his turn to show them what the one true God of heaven and earth could do. He built up a huge altar with twelve stones representing the twelve tribes of Jacob. He had the servants dig a trench around the altar and place wood on it. Then he did something strange. He asked the servants to drench the altar with water, not once, not twice, but *three times*. The Bible says the trenches were filled with water. There could be no thought that some trick had started this fire, since wet wood would be impossible to burn. Elijah begins to pray his simple prayer and asks God to bring down fire and show His almighty power.

Instantly, God rained down fire. The Bible says the fire was so big and hot that nothing was left, not the sacrifice, wood, stones, water, even the dirt. The land was beyond recognition. That is power, God's true power. The people immediately started proclaiming, "The Lord, He is God!"

Now that God had won, Elijah commanded the people to get rid of the idols and false prophets. Elijah had them taken down to the valley and slaughtered. Nothing competes with God. *Read 1 Kings 18:38–40.*

Elijah then told Ahab to go home and prepare for rain. Remember, it hadn't rained in three years. Ahab left while Elijah went back up to Mt. Carmel and prayed. He asked God to bring rain. He asked his servant to look on the ocean waters to see if there was a rain cloud. The servant came back and reported that there was not. This happened *seven times*, and the seventh time, the rain cloud appeared. It was small, but it was there. Seven is the Lord's number for completion, and it came to pass. Elijah was happy to see rain and God's faithfulness. He was so excited he ran back to the palace on foot, beating the chariots by twenty miles or so.

Jezebel was *very* angry when she found out that God had rained down fire and humiliated her priests and then had them killed. She began to falsely prophesy that Elijah would be dead by the next day. She pretended to have supernatural power. She didn't; she just had a strong hatred for righteous people. That is a characteristic of the Jezebel spirit today. When Elijah found out that Jezebel wanted his head, however, he fled. He was at this point fed up, tired of dealing with her. He wanted to die and asked God to take him. He even wanted to kill himself, quit being a prophet. He was depressed, lonely, and full of fear—even after the great victory. He cried to God until he collapsed. He was done. Graciously, God came down and met Elijah in his need. He told Elijah He wanted three things from him before he could die.

The angel of the Lord strengthened Elijah because God had another journey for him to do. God told Elijah that He would never leave him and reminded him of all he had seen. He could survive the wrath of Jezebel. God would be with him. All this took place and the day had passed. Jezebel's prophecy of having Elijah's head by sundown had failed; he was alive.

God needed Elijah to do three things before he would take him to heaven:

1.   Anoint Hazael king over Syria (Aram)
2.   Anoint Jehu (Jay-hu) king over Israel
3.   Anoint Elisha as his successor

God still needed to deal with Ahab for the stolen vineyard. So Elijah went to King Ahab and said to him, "You know God sees all things." He allowed him to repent for stealing the vineyard and having Naboth murdered. He prophesied that when Ahab and Jezebel died, they wouldn't get a proper burial. The dogs would come and lick their blood. No honor or tombstone for them. Ahab did end up repenting and God had mercy on him (1 Kings 21:27-29 NIV), but he still died in battle. Jehu, who was a ruthless soldier, had been commanded to get justice for Naboth's family by destroying the rest of Ahab's family, including Jezebel. You need a spirit of Jehu when dealing with Jezebel spirit.

Years later, Jehu drove an arrow through the heart of Jezebel's son, who was reigning as king, and killed him. Jezebel, hearing the news, and in a downward spiral, almost ritualistically painted her face, knowing she was near certain death. Looking down arrogantly from her bedroom window, she taunted Jehu. Jehu told the eunuchs in her room to throw her from the window. She died from the fall, most likely, but just in case, horses trampled over her and then dogs ripped her apart and drank her blood. There was nothing left of her body except her hands and feet and skull. The word from God was right. She would never be laid to rest and have a proper burial. Surely she resides in hell. This spirit is linked to possessiveness, jealousy, sexuality, manipulation, and control.

Are you under the influence of a Jezebel spirit or is someone you know?

First, before going into the signs of the "spirit of Jezebel," it is important to debunk myths of Jezebel:

1. This spirit is not only assigned or manifested in women; it is a spirit of control and sexuality that both men and women can be influenced by.
2. "Jezebel" is a territorial principality, which means a second heaven (not the inner court of heaven) demon.
3. In the book *Jezebel's Puppets*, Jennifer LeClaire describes the spirit that dwelled in Jezebel to be one of the most wicked, roaming the earth for thousands

of years, looking to seduce people into ungodly things.
4. A big red flag that this spirit is manifesting is control and seduction.

Ten Characteristics of the Jezebel Spirit

1. *Jezebel's ultimate goal is always to control.* The Jezebel spirit is always motivated by its agenda, which it relentlessly pursues.
2. *The Jezebel spirit attacks, dominates, or manipulates especially male authority.*
   Queen Jezebel usurped the political authority of the kingdom. This spirit's goal is to conquer or neutralize the prophet because a discerning leader is its greatest enemy.
3. *Jezebel causes fear, flight, and discouragement.*
   This spirit often causes a spiritual leader to flee from his appointed place by engaging in character assassination and ruining his reputation.
4. *People under Jezebel's influence are natural leaders, although often covertly.*
   The Jezebel spirit attempts to seek out people of influence to win their ear, gain credibility, and win endorsement for their toxic cause.
5. *People under Jezebel's influence are often insecure and wounded, with pronounced egocentric needs.*
   They are often trying to fill a love deficit. People under Jezebel's control always have deep, unhealed wounds from sources such as rejection, resistance, fear, insecurity, self-preservation, and bitterness. These in turn spread their defilement to many.
6. *The Jezebel spirit functions subtlety and deceptively.*
   People controlled by Jezebel use flattery to win you over to their domination. Jezebel spirits are masters of manipulation, operating using guilt and undermining or discrediting another's influence.

Those under Jezebel's control use flirtation and are extremely jealous of anyone they perceive to be a threat.

7. *Ultimately, people under Jezebel's influence are proud, independent, and rebellious.*
   Rebellion is the sin of witchcraft (1 Samuel 15:23) and will attempt to control others through any means other than the Holy Spirit.

8. *It takes an Ahab to let a Jezebel spirit operate unchallenged.*
   Those under Jezebel's influence do not operate without someone who is under an Ahab spirit's influence that enables them to function.

9. *A Jezebel spirit is always in alignment with a religious spirit.*
   Both Jezebel in the Old Testament and the one mentioned in Revelation in the New Testament operated under the cover of religion. Its religious deeds are done for all to see. True and pure spiritual gifts attract people to Jesus, not to the people who exercise the gifts.

10. *The families of people under Jezebel's influence are often out of order.*
    Those under Jezebel's influence control their partners and cause their children to take sides. The children grow up insecure, disrespect their fathers, feel manipulated, and become distrustful of true authority.
    (Source: https://ifapray.org/blog/10-characteristics-of-the-jezebel-spirit/)

Verses about Jezebel:

> ➤ Leviticus 24:16
> ➤ Deuteronomy 19:15
> ➤ 1 Kings 16:31, 30–37; 18:22–31, 44–45; 21:4, 7, 25; 19:4, 18

- ➢ 2 Kings 9:22, 26
- ➢ Psalm 35:13
- ➢ Proverbs 1:24–26
- ➢ Matthew 23:37

Questions about Jezebel:

1. Read 1 Kings 21:25. What is said of Ahab in this passage?
2. In your opinion, what motivated Jezebel?
3. Why do you think she painted her face just before her death?
4. What was your biggest takeaway from her life story?
5. What is God teaching us with Jezebel?

Fill in the blanks (use the ESV translation):

2 Kings 9:37. "And the corpse of _____shall be as _____ on the face of the field in the territory of Jezreel, so that no one can say, '_____.'"

1 Kings 18:4 "And when Jezebel cut off the _____ of the LORD, _____ took a hundred prophets and hid them by fifties in a _____ and fed them with bread and water."

Personal reflections:

Do I have the Jezebel spirit operating in my life? If so, how will I repent and change my ways to rebuke the spirit?

_____

_____

Do I have an idol in my life that is in position over Christ? If so, what is it?

_____

_____

Can I relate to the weariness of Elijah in this story? If so, how can I be refreshed by living waters?

_____

_____

Is there evidence of the religious spirit in my own life?

_____

_____

What did Jesus say about Jezebel in Revelation 2:20?

_____

_____

_____

Huldah

A woman who rebukes a nation back into God's grace

The story of Huldah is mentioned in 2 Kings 22. Huldah (hull-duh) was a prophetess; she spoke for God.

Josiah came into kingship at eight years old. His reign started so young because his father was so evil. the Lord only let him reign for a few years, then killed him, leaving Josiah to step into his kingship. After eight years of being king, at age sixteen, Josiah sought the Lord and asked Him for advice. He noticed his whole government was in disarray. He began the task of dismantling the mess his father had made. Some of us are dismantling the mess of a previous generation and can learn from Josiah's example. Generational sins are real and affect generations until they are dealt with and repented for.

At Josiah's command, the temple of the Lord was being cleaned and repaired. A book was found. It had been hidden by a priest years before and was a copy of the law of God that Moses had written. *Read 2 Kings 22:8–10.*

As they read the book, the priests realized the mass purging needed to be done on a great level. They brought the book of the law to King Josiah, who read it and realized they were in a lot of sin. He asks the priests to seek the Lord for him and let him know what God reveals because of the level of sin the nation had fallen into. It is interesting to note that the king, his noblemen, and the priests did not seek the Lord directly. They did not even try. Instead, they went to see Huldah, the prophetess. *Read 2 Kings 22:14–18.*

Huldah said that the Lord was angry with them for having other idols and gods before Him and using their hands for selfish works and burning incense to other gods. God is a jealous God and will not tolerate coming second to anything. Just like a husband does not deserve a second place to another man, God deserves the first place with us; He deserves our praise and honor. But the people had long forgotten Him. Huldah was bold enough and had power and authority in the Lord enough to rebuke the government officials and even priests for disobedience to God. She spoke a giant rebuke to all of Judah. Then, she went on to offer a kind word, recorded in 2 Kings 22:19-20 NIV. She told them that because they had humbled themselves, repented for their wickedness, cried out to God, and tore their clothes, God will have mercy. He had heard their cries. She proclaimed that the Lord said, yes, there will be a calamity over the nation of Judah, but it will not happen in the time of Josiah.

Huldah stepped into prophesying and did so in balance. She was able to speak and rebuke the nation for their sin, but also to offer God's peace and give encouragement to the people. King Josiah then gathered his people and said, "Let's renew the covenant with the Lord and tear down all the idols and incense burning. Let's repent and turn from our sin." Huldah's boldness to speak the truth brought an entire nation into repentance. God is even now raising men and women who are in line with His truth and have a level of boldness and authority through a relationship with Him that will speak truth into people's lives. Because of that, they will repent. The truth will set you free.

If you are thinking that you will never be as bold as to speak up for God in front of people, you can. Proverbs 18:16 says that a man's gift makes a way for him to come before great men. Work on your gift, become excellent at whatever it is. Huldah was the wife of Shallum, the man in charge of the king's wardrobe. She cared for her husband dearly. Yet her marriage did not stand in the way of her living out her calling. The Israelites currently were not serving God; they were serving idols. They had turned away from God's laws that were given by Moses centuries before. They were not faithful to God. God had told them to hide the flaws in their hearts and pass them onto their children, but they had failed. *Read Deuteronomy 30:14.*

When the men came looking for Huldah to speak a word over the situation, she wasn't caught up in flattery or vanity. She knew the Lord needed her obedience. When the king read the book of the law of Moses and found out how far the nation had strayed from God, he was ashamed. The Bible says, "He was ashamed about the sin of his people." (Exodus 32:30-32). He understood that the situation was very serious; he feared the wrath of God.

Since the time of David and Solomon, they had departed from their covenant with God. They had backslid as a nation and allowed the compromise of culture to become their way of life. Jesus reminds us of the danger of compromising with the world. Huldah carried out her calling and duties with excellence, fearlessness, and boldness in the Lord. It was the first time in many years that Judah had a king who wholeheartedly served the Lord.

God often partnered with men and women in the Old Testament to accomplish His will. In the New Testament, He sent His son. When the priests finally spoke to Huldah, she predicted a terrible message of judgment for the nation including its downfall. *Read 2 Chronicles 34:25.*

God not only spoke judgment through Huldah but also grace. He saw Josiah's heart for Him and His scriptures, so he postponed judgment until after Josiah's death. God delayed judgment because of one man's honor; how true that can be for today. After the revelation of King Josiah's heart and repentance, he tried to turn the people from their wicked ways. They cleaned out all the idols from the land, fixed the temple, and put God back as first love, His rightful place.

As certain as disobedience is followed by God's curse, so obedience is always followed by God's blessing. Not only was Josiah's life changed after this word through Huldah, but an entire nation was transformed. Huldah was prepared to prophesy when God needed her, no matter what. We can assess our own lives for the same calling and obedience.

Verses about Huldah:

> ➢ Exodus 12:1–17;15:20; 23:14–15
> ➢ Deuteronomy 6:6–9; 7:6; 28:1–64; 30:14
> ➢ Joshua 1:8
> ➢ Judges 4:4
> ➢ 2 Kings 23:4–8
> ➢ 2 Chronicles 34:1–19, 23–28; 33:1–25; 34:30
> ➢ Psalm 1:1–13
> ➢ Jeremiah 22:29, 25:3–7, 29:19
> ➢ Hosea 4:6
> ➢ Zephaniah 1:1–6

Questions about Huldah:

1. Why was Huldah chosen to announce judgment? What proved she spoke in the name of God?
2. Why was God's judgment held until Josiah died?
3. What changes took place after Huldah spoke?
4. What effect does God's word have on your life?

Fill in the blanks (use the ESV translation):

2 Kings 22:14. "So Hilkiah the priest, and Ahikam, and Achbor, and Shaphan, and Asaiah went to _____the prophetess, the wife of _____ the son of Tikvah, son of Harhas, keeper of the wardrobe (now she lived in Jerusalem in the Second Quarter), and they _____ with her."

2 Kings 22:17. "Because they have _____ and have made offerings to other gods, that they might provoke me to anger with all the work of their hands, therefore my _____ will be kindled against this place, and it will not be quenched."

Personal reflections:

What was God's two-fold task to Huldah?

_____

Do I possess the boldness of God in situations where He needs me to be bold?

_____

_____

Do I live a life of conviction like Josiah? Does what grieve the Lord grieve me also?

_____

_____

Write Isaiah 65:3 and why this would grieve the Lord.

_____

_____

How can I apply to my life not only Huldah's rebuke but her grace?

_____

_____

Lydia

A woman with a heart after God's will who displayed great leadership

Lydia's story unfolds in the book of Acts. Studying Acts, we see the power of the Holy Spirit and what He accomplishes with our partnership. There are only a few verses that mention a woman named Lydia, but those verses have a great impact. She is first mentioned praying by the riverbank in the city of Philippi. She responded to the gospel and started a relationship with Christ. She offered her home to host small groups of believers. She was an example of responding with an open heart to God's spirit leading and moving in her life. *Read Acts 16:13–15.*

Paul had just taken his second missionary trip, working from Turkey down to Philippi in Macedonia and then Rome. Timothy joined Paul as they journeyed, sharing the gospel. The Holy Spirit had stopped them from going where they had intended to go next, Asia, and sent them to Macedonia instead. God is intentional in His open and closed doors. We must be sensitive to His workings, even when we do not understand.

Paul and his apprentices went to the river one Sabbath day where women were praying. One of the women they met at the river was Lydia. She sold purple dye from Thyatira.

She was later baptized and used her home as a house of prayer. She had financial means and used this gift to honor God. When Paul later got out of prison, he went to Lydia's house. She chose to be used by God and use her possessions for God's purposes, not her own.

Lydia was saved as an adult, so hers is a story of conversion and redemption from her past unsaved life to new life in Christ. Much like the other women studied, she shows us the power of new life in Christ. She was a prayer warrior and intercessor at heart. These women met at the river to pray, and she was faithful about going.

There was no synagogue in the city she lived in; it was primarily a Gentile city. When Paul arrived, he wanted to go to the synagogue but was informed they did not have one. It was a government requirement that there had to be ten Jewish men to establish a synagogue in any city. This city was a city that did not follow God's ways; it was pagan at its core. The people of the city worshipped the pagan goddess, Diana. These practices were troublesome to Lydia, who had converted to Judaism.

She was searching for meaning and depth in her life, and the answers only come when we seek God. God promises if you seek Him, you will find Him. Once Jesus came and died in our place, the perfection God was seeking from us was met by Jesus; He bridged the gap for us. Now, we can come to God as we are. As a good father, He takes joy in His children coming to Him with all our needs.

Learning God's character and nature is a duty and privilege of the believer. Once you understand His heart you can come into repentance knowing He is a merciful and just God who always gives us time to repent before His judgment.

At the time of Lydia's story, it had been about twelve years since Jesus had died and risen from the grave. The church was very young, with a lot of new believers. Lydia was one of them. We see God's providence in this story and the leading of the Holy Spirit. *Read Jeremiah 17:7.*

Lydia is only mentioned by name three times in scripture, but God uses this ordinary woman to make a great impact. She is instrumental in starting the church in Philippi. As mentioned previously, she was from the city of Thyatira, a small, rich city known for its dye facilities and cloth making. It also had guilds for ironworkers, wool and leather workers, and potters, but the most popular were coppersmiths and dye makers. She was a textile merchant and still maintained her connections in Thyatira.

The color purple in the Bible is connected to royalty. In Exodus, Moses and Aaron had this color as their curtain in the tent meetings. In the book of Kings, the kings of Midian wore purple robes. In Rome, purple was associated with royalty and by law, only those of high rank were allowed to wear it. After whipping Jesus nearly to death, the soldiers placed a purple robe over him as if to mock him, believing he was not royalty. Little did they know that Jesus is the King of Kings and Lord of Lords, the ultimate royal.

Selling purple cloth would have made Lydia a wealthy woman of that time. We do not know if she was married or had children, as scripture does not mention a family, but many scholars believe she was likely a widow. It does mention that she worshipped God faithfully.

She was an entrepreneur who was blessed with great means, and she used that for the Lord. She invited people back to her home, including Paul and Timothy and friends, for fellowship and a meal. She was welcoming and people loved going to her home because they felt her kind heart, but also the presence of Jesus there. God used her to minister to people in her city and home. Her circle of influence became greater as she was obedient in showing hospitality.

Read Romans 8:31. Lydia was a person who loved the Lord and helped establish the church where she lived. She used her means to help her ministry of serving and leading people to Christ. She listened to the teaching and instruction of Paul and lived a redeemed life that had a great influence on the people around her.

Verses about Lydia:

> ➤ Jeremiah 17:7
> ➤ Acts 16
> ➤ Romans 8:31

Questions about Lydia:

1. Is there someone in your life who displays the love of Christ and has influenced you in a good way?
2. Why do you think the Holy Spirit directed Paul and his team to Philippi?
3. Why is Lydia a good example of a Christian entrepreneur?
4. How does Romans 8:31 resemble Lydia's life?

Fill in the blanks (use the ESV translation):

Acts 16:14. "One who heard us was a woman named Lydia, from the city of _____, a seller of _____ goods, who was a _____ of God. The Lord opened her heart to pay attention to what was said by _____."

Acts 16:15. "And after she was _____, and her household as well, she urged us, saying, 'If you have

judged me to be _____ to the Lord, come to my
_____and stay.' And she prevailed upon us."

Personal reflections:

Is there evidence of the fruit of Christ in my new life in Him?
If yes, what are they?

_____

_____

Name some other people in the Bible who owned their
businesses.

_____

Write out Ezekiel 22:30–31. What does it say about prayer?

_____

_____

How can I use my gifts and possessions to serve the body
of Christ better?

_____

_____

Salome

A mother who put her children first

Salome (sal-o-me) was the mother of John and James and a follower of Christ, and possibly sister to the mother of Jesus, Mary. That would make her Jesus's aunt. She was one of the women present at the crucifixion and went to Jesus's tomb to prepare his body with spices. She was also one of four women mentioned when references were given to the women who followed and ministered with Jesus.

Salome's husband was Zebedee, a successful fisherman. When his sons left to follow Jesus, the business suffered a bit. He now relied on workers, but Salome and Zebedee were still very happy for John and James. Salome's motivations, after Jesus announced his upcoming death, were selfish and only concerned with the well-being of her sons. Because their hopes were dependent on them, she began to worry.

It was nearly Passover, and she couldn't wait to tell Jesus something. She knew Jesus would be killed soon and this doom was plaguing Salome's thoughts. He told his disciples that he would be killed and rise on the third day. (Remember that everything we go through in life, Including shame and rejection, were also experienced by Jesus himself.)

Salome decided to make sure her sons had a secure future after Jesus died. When Jesus asked what he could do for her, she replied "Grant that one of these two sons of mine may sit at your right and the other at your left in your kingdom" (Matthew 20:21 NIV). Did she even ask herself once she had spoken those words, *Am I sounding selfish?* We don't know. The innocence of God was about to die, and her first thought was about her sons. Maybe this was motherly pride. But her sons did not correct her. They wanted to know that their suffering would be rewarded.

God's love doesn't work this way. The Bible says Salome was also the mouthpiece for her sons. This means she spoke for them instead of them speaking from their own experiences with Jesus. The Lord must have felt deserted by His best friends, John and James. Later, the other disciples were furious over this. It was clear that John and James thought higher of themselves than the others.

Jesus did not reprimand Salome; He forgave her. He knew that even though she had shortcomings, she had faith. Jesus knew her heart was to see her sons be close to Jesus and He appreciated that loyalty. Jesus was to establish the heavenly kingdom, not an earthly one. He knew the gate to that kingdom was the gate of suffering. Salome was there a few days later at the foot of the cross and heard His cry to heaven. John and James knew there was suffering for Jesus. They decided after seeing Him resurrected that this was their destiny on earth too—to share the gospel.

We are unsure if Salome was around to see James get killed by Herod, and John was exiled at the end of his life for the gospel. They were not surrendered to the earthly kings, but they knew the one true king, Jesus. Jesus asked John to care for His mother after His death. Serving, like suffering, is a pillar on which the everlasting kingdom of God has been constructed. Mothers must learn not to be too hasty in their prayers for their children; they must be unselfish.

Verses about Salome:

> ➤ Matthew 19:2; 20:21–22
> ➤ Mark 10: 35–45; 15:40–41; 1:11
> ➤ John 6:15; 19:25–27
> ➤ Acts 1:6; 12:1–2
> ➤ Hebrews 2:10; 5:8
> ➤ 1 Peter 4:12–13
> ➤ Revelation 1:9

Questions about Salome

1. Why did James and John not say anything to correct their mother?
2. What were Salome's motives, in your opinion?
3. In this example, what can you learn from the word of God that can be applied to your life?

Fill in the blanks (use the ESV translation):

1 Peter 4:12–13. "Beloved, do not be _____ at the fiery _____when it comes upon you to _____, as though something strange were happening to you. But rejoice insofar as you share Christ's _____, that you may also rejoice and be glad when his _____is revealed."

Personal reflections:

What is wrong with motherly pride?

_____

Why were the disciples always in competition with each other for Jesus's affections and "first place"?

_____

_____

Write Luke 13:30 and reflect.

_____

_____

In my walk with Christ do I strive? Do I fight by works to feel closer to Him? If yes, what does the Bible say about works?

_____

_____

Week Six Review

Review your Bible verses for each woman. Pray over new revelation through the Word.

Weekly Challenge:

Ask God to help you take the righteous path in all decisions with the leadership of the Holy Spirit. Ask Him to remove all wickedness from your heart and to search your heart daily.

Prayer:

Heavenly Father, I come before Your throne of grace asking to be cleansed from my sin. I do not want to have self-serving, selfish motives. I know Your word says the least among us is the greatest and to serve Your kingdom. I want to place You as of first in my life, my priorities, and affections because that is what You are, first and deserving of all my praise. Help me to be transformed into a servant of the king. Open doors where I can show my love to others and bring opportunities where I can bless others. Let me respond well when You bring someone into my life that speaks a rebuke or correction over me. Let me respond in obedience, knowing You are refining me and with obedience comes Your cover and blessing. As I press into You, Lord, I choose to die to self and die to the love of the things of this world, as they can offer me nothing. I choose You, Lord, in everything I do. Help me to look more like You, Jesus, each day. In Your holy name, I pray this, amen.

Weekly Declaration:

I declare that I am moving at the pace of God's grace. I will not run ahead and rush the promise He has for me. I will trust Him, honor Him, and abide inside His will. I will have everything He has promised me. God is faithful. God won't fail me. His word is true, unfailing, and forever. The thing God has spoken over me will come true. It will come to pass. God's promise is coming. This is my declaration.

WOW Week Seven

Prayer: Heavenly Father, I pray that You fill this room with Your transforming presence, so I leave this space changed. Allow the Holy Spirit to stir within me a desire for righteousness so I will walk upright in Your eyes. Let me know if all things are possible with You. I want to connect to your Spirit. Remove all distractions from my mind as I concentrate on You. In Jesus's name, amen.

This week we will study the lives of Claudia, Joanna, and Mary of Jerusalem.

Claudia

A woman devoted to God and establishing the church

In the book of Acts, it is recorded that Paul was writing letters to churches. Some churches were having challenges and he was addressing how to biblically solve them. The church was new and needed guidance and structure on how to follow the Lord. Paul was instrumental in helping us understand the structure of the church—from how to dress to tithing, conflict resolution, five-fold ministry (Ephesians 4:11-13 NIV), etc.

People of this time were learning what it meant to live holy and be Christian. The Bible is about righteousness. Righteousness is the ticket into heaven. We must be in *right standing* with God to enter into His holiness. Sanctification helps us obtain righteousness through Jesus, repentance, and His blood.

Paul had an apprentice, Timothy. In one letter he added his greetings (which he often did) from specific people; he mentioned three men, then Claudia. She was the only woman mentioned in this group in this greeting. *Read 2 Timothy 4:21.*

Claudia was honored by Paul and named for her missionary work in the early church in this particular letter—much like the deaconess Phoebe, who was also instrumental in the success of the early church.

Claudia could have responded poorly, noticing she was mentioned fourth after the men. But she was noted. It is human instinct to want to be recognized, whether it is as part of a team or for our individual achievements. But God sees things differently than we do. He is not attached to the earthly perspective as we are; His is a heavenly one. We are not storing up treasures on earth but in heaven. How we handle our temples (our bodies), use our gifts, and manage this life directly affects our authority and gloried bodies in eternity. *Read 1 Timothy 6:18–19 and Matthew 6:21.*

Not many facts can be gathered about Claudia. We can deduce her geographic location and that she was a Christian woman. Her heart was devoted to Paul, and she knew Timothy. Paul sent his letter from Rome, where he was awaiting trial under Emperor Nero. Because Paul sent greetings from Claudia and other saints, we can assume that Claudia was in Rome with Paul at that time. We also know that she was fighting for Christ's message because of her relationship to the other men whom Paul names: Eubulus and Pudens, and Linus, who became the first bishop of Rome after the apostles. Claudia mentions all three.

Paul does not mention everyone by name, but, since Claudia is among those he does name, we know that she remained devoted to Paul throughout his imprisonment. Timothy must have known Claudia as well since she sends her greetings with the rest.

Loyalty is important to God, and it is written about in many stories of the Bible. Loyalty and love are intertwined and flow from the heart. *Read Proverbs 4:23.*

Verses about Claudia:

> ➤ Proverbs 3:3; 4:23
> ➤ Matthew 6:21
> ➤ 1 Timothy 6:18–19
> ➤ 2 Timothy 4:21

Questions about Claudia:

1. Can you share a time you had an important task to do that was entrusted to you?
2. Put in your own words what loyalty means to you.
3. Why did Paul mention Claudia among his loyal friends?
4. Have you remained loyal to a friend, and why? Or if not, then why not?

Fill in the blanks (use the ESV translation):

2 Timothy 4:21. "Do your best to _____ before winter. Eubulus sends greetings to you, as do Pudens and _____ and Claudia and all the brothers."

Acts 9:31. "So the church throughout all _____ and Galilee and Samaria had peace and was being _____. And walking in the _____ of the Lord and in the comfort of the Holy Spirit, it _____."

Personal reflections:

What is the five-fold ministry? Briefly describe each one.

_____

Am I using my gifts to serve the kingdom of God usefully? If not, how can I do better?

_____

Write out Proverbs 4:23.

_____

Why is it important to honor the people who serve with you?

_____

_____

Joanna

A woman delivered by Jesus

Joanna appears only in the gospel of Luke, the book in the New Testament that records the most women and their stories. As with the gospel of Mark, which talks about Salome, Luke mentions stories and names that do not appear in the other gospels.

Joanna appears alongside Mary Magdalene and Mother Mary to embalm Jesus, which they did not get to do. By the time they arrived at the tomb on the third day, He had risen from the dead. Amen!

Joanna most likely knew the disciples, as she knew and followed Jesus. The four gospels are each slightly different from each other because of the authors' various perspectives. Another interesting thing we know about Joanna, like Mary Magdalene, is that Jesus cast out demons from her. Deliverance ministry is necessary for most Christians who have picked up demons through open doors of sin, sex, and generational curses before they were saved. Most saved Christians still need ongoing deliverance. It was a big part of Jesus's ministry while on earth. It could be assumed that when people were getting healed by Jesus, it often was deliverance from demonic oppression.

Jesus became Joanna's Lord and teacher and she cared for Him. *Read Luke 8:3.*

We know that Joanna was married to a man named Chuza, who was the manager of Herod's household. Despite the close association that Chuza (and thus her entire family) had with Herod, Joanna did not let that stop her from following Jesus Christ and doing what was right in God's eyes. We can learn from Joanna's example of creating a godly inner circle. She not only followed Christ's teaching and was there at the cross, but she was planning to anoint His body with spices after His death. She surrounded herself with a tribe of women who would support and edify her faith. *Read Proverbs 12: 26.*

The same is true for us today. We need to allow God to bring women into our lives like He brought Susanna, Mary, and Mother Mary into Joanna's life. Women who will give us biblical advice, support, and love us, but more importantly, pray for us. A big part of God's blessing for our lives is who He brings into it. *Read Proverbs 13:20.*

Ask God for wise, true disciples of the faith to come into your life and make the connections. This is key for our faith journey here on earth. Evaluate your life and inner circle and surrender it to God. *Read Psalm 18:24.*

Verses about Joanna:

- ➢ Psalm 18:24
- ➢ Proverbs 12:26; 13:20
- ➢ Luke 8:3

Questions about Joanna:

1. Have you been in a situation where you could have influenced events for the good, but didn't?
2. Have you asked God for godly women friendships?
3. Who is in your inner circle and are they a source of righteousness?

Fill in the blanks (use the ESV translation):

Proverbs 13:20. "Whoever walks with the _____ becomes wise, but the _____ of fools will suffer _____."

Psalm 18:24. "So the LORD has _____ me according to my righteousness, according to the _____ of my _____ in his sight."

Personal reflections:

Do I have a godly inner circle? If not, why is that?

_____

_____

Why is deliverance ministry so important to the Christian?

_____

_____

Why must I put what God wants first over what man wants of me?

_____

_____

Write out Jeremiah 17:7 and consider if you are following this scripture.

_____

_____

Mary of Jerusalem

A woman who made her home a church

The book of Acts talks a lot about the city of Jerusalem. The early church met in homes then, much as it will be in the final days. One of the homes was Mary of Jerusalem's house. She held small group meetings in her home where people came to worship the Lord in secret. It was a time of persecution for the Christians. Herod was killing the disciples, and they had to seek the Lord in secret.

Mary was drawn toward God and wasn't afraid to risk her life; she wanted to serve the Lord. At the time, Jewish leaders were jealous of the apostles, who were doing signs and wonders for God. This is why they were putting believers in prison, like Peter who had been arrested by Herod. Mary was a biblical woman, and it was written that she influenced Jerusalem. She was also the mother of John, also known as John Mark and likely the author of the book of Mark, according to the second-century Christian writer Papias.

We do know Mary was wealthy and had a large home that became the meeting place for the early Christians of Jerusalem. This was the home where they met to learn the word and to worship. However, as much as we know about Mary of Jerusalem, her home, and her relationship with the

Lord, the Bible never mentions her husband; she may have been a widow.

At this time, the culture had public hatred for Jesus and His followers; the apostle James had already been executed, and there was the expectation that Peter would die for his devotion as well. The persecutors made a point to kill Jesus's followers brutally and very publicly. Satan's plan has always been to punish and embarrass believers and try to cause them to hide in shame. That is why the Bible says not to be ashamed of the gospel. Jesus later said if you deny Him, He will deny you in front of His Father (Matthew 10:33 NIV).

Peter had been arrested. The believers gathered at Mary's home that night to pray for him, no doubt. In prison, he had many guards watching him to prevent any escape. His hands and feet were in chains, and he was in the deepest part of the prison. Read Acts 12:1–19.

The people who met at Mary's house believed in the righteousness of God's people and the power of the supernatural. While they prayed, an angel of the Lord appeared to Peter in the prison and shook the chains from his hands and feet. The angel told Peter to get up and follow him. He thought it was a vision until they had passed through all the gates and the angel disappeared. Once he realized he was awake and freed, in amazement he ran for the shelter of Mary's house where he knew the church would be praying for him. Remember the powerful words of Psalm 91, which says, "I will answer them that call on the Lord" (Psalm 91:15 NIV).

After the Holy Spirit came upon the world after Pentecost, people collected their resources to help the needy. Mary did not sell her home and use the money for the poor, however. Instead, she kept her home as a house to be used by the Lord. She was a biblical example of godly independence and leadership. Mary understood there are many ways to serve the Lord, and she listened to what He was speaking to her and allowed her home and the gifts of the spirit to be a lighthouse to other Christians.

Mary had her function within the church. Peter went on to share the gospel, and Mary remained close to Christ and lived her life as a woman of God. *Read Acts 12:25.*

The Bible only mentions Mary once and the emphasis is not on her, but on her home. Some say it was in her home where Jesus had the Last Supper with His disciples before His crucifixion. The rest of Mary's story is unknown. One day the records of the good deeds of men and women will be opened in the courts of heaven, and it will become clear to all the saints of heaven how important Mary of Jerusalem was to God's plan.

Read 1 Peter 5:13. It could be that the Mark this scripture is referring to is John Mark, who was Barnabas's sister's son. His mother's name was Mary. It was a popular name in that culture and the best way to differentiate them is to follow their lineages.

Verses about Mary of Jerusalem:

- ➤ 1 Kings 17:7–16
- ➤ Isaiah 62:7
- ➤ Malachi 3:16
- ➤ Matthew 2:16; 18:19–20; 21:22
- ➤ Luke 2:25–38; 8:3
- ➤ John 11:54; 12:1–11
- ➤ Acts 8:2; Acts 3:6–8; 5:15; 12:12; 12:25; 5:7; 7:57–60
- ➤ Hebrews 7:25
- ➤ James 5:16

Questions about Mary of Jerusalem:

1. How did Mary feel about her home being used for God?
2. How does the Bible tell us to respond to adversity?
3. Why was Mary so beloved?
4. Why do you think Mary kept her house as a place of worship instead of selling it?
5. Do you have a mother figure that influenced you for Christ? Who was she?

Fill in the blanks (use the ESV translation):

James 5:16 "Therefore, _____ your sins to one another and pray for one another, that you may be _____ The prayer of a _____ person has great power as it is _____."

Hebrews 7:25. "Consequently, he is able to save to the uttermost those who _____ to God through him, since he always _____to make _____for them."

Personal reflections:

What are some ways I can use my home to honor Christ?

_____

_____

When I face hard times, what is my default reaction? If it is not trusting God, how can I do better to trust Him?

_____

_____

Write out Isaiah 43:2–3 and what this means to you.

_____

_____

What does the Bible say about using your (spiritual) gifts for the church?

_____

_____

_____

Week Seven Review

Review your Bible verses for each woman. Pray over new revelation through the word.

Weekly Challenge:

Ask God to help you choose righteousness in every situation. Cast out and rebuke the lying spirit that stirs up in you. Ask Him to cultivate loyalty and dependency on Him for all things.

Prayer:

Heavenly Father, I come before Your throne of grace surrendering myself to You, Lord. You can have my talents, gifts, and the whole being to glorify Your holy name. I want to be a person You trust, a person of righteousness. I want to know Your law and obey it, but also accept and know the love and transforming power of Jesus. I want to remain in You, Jesus, because I know apart from You, I can do nothing, accomplish nothing. I ask the Holy Spirit to help me become more like Christ and daily lead and teach me my errors and transform my heart. I know the heart is wicked and I cannot trust it, but with You leading me, Lord, I know I can. Search me, Lord, and remove anything that does not please You. Let me desire things that You desire and not what the culture predicts. Let me stand on Your word and Your truth and be strengthened by it every day. I love You, Jesus; I want my life to honor You. In Jesus's name, I pray this, amen.

Weekly Declaration:

I declare that I will choose faith over fear. I will remember that it's God's perfect love that casts out fear in all situations. I will not make decisions based on the world's view but God's view. I will meditate on positive things, pure things, and godly things. My mind is set on what God says about me, for I know His plan is good. This is my declaration.

WOW Week Eight

Prayer: Lord, I invite You into this space to be seated in the highest place of honor. I exalt You and desire to learn Your ways. Plant me by Your living waters so that I will never thirst and will always bear good fruit. Let my life be influenced by these stories in a transforming way. I invite the Holy Spirit's transforming power into this space and into my heart to make me be more like Christ. In Your Holy name, Jesus, amen.

This week we will study the lives of Priscilla and Lois and Eunice.

Priscilla

A woman and wife devoted to the gospel and starting the early church

Priscilla was married to Aquila. They were missionaries preaching the gospel in Greece and Asia. Her story unfolds in the book of Acts. She was exiled from Rome with her husband when the Roman emperor Claudius issued a decree expelling all Jews from the city. She and Aquila were tentmakers by trade and so was Paul. This was probably how their friendship started when Paul met them in Corinth. *Read Acts 18:1–3.*

They worked with Paul in establishing church plants. Paul moved on to other places, whereas Priscilla and her husband stayed in Corinth for a while and then went on to Ephesus. In Ephesus, they met a young man who only knew of the baptism of John the Baptist and a bit of the Bible. His name was Apollos. Priscilla and Aquila gave him the context of the whole gospel and introduced him to the story of Jesus, quietly discipling him. Later, he too became a powerful evangelist. *Read Acts 18:26.*

When Paul wrote one of his letters, he mentioned Priscilla and Aquila as fellow laborers in the cause for Christ. *Read Romans 16:3–4.*

Later, they moved back to Rome and started a church there with the aid of Timothy (Paul's apprentice). Paul writes a letter to that church too. *Read 2 Timothy 4:19.*

The Bible does not ever mention Priscilla and Aquila as individuals, but rather as a team. Contrary to the cultural norm, her name was mentioned first. We can assume it is because she took the lead in their ministry, or that Paul wanted to validate her contribution and not place her second.

While in Ephesus, Priscilla and Aquila started another home church. When they eventually moved back to Italy, they started yet another home church (second church plant) in Rome. They were church planters, leaders, and true evangelists for God.

God is looking for people willing to do His will and share His good news of salvation. This couple did not have a position, power, or a tremendous amount of money. What they did have was a tentmaking business, a good work ethic, good public speaking and discipleship skills, a great understanding of the Bible and Jesus—and willing hearts. They are a great example of what a married couple can do when they are united with God in their ministry and calling. *Read Proverbs 3:6.*

Verses about Priscilla:

- ➤ Proverbs 3:6
- ➤ Acts 18:1–3, 26
- ➤ Romans 16:3–4
- ➤ 2 Timothy 4:19

Questions about Priscilla:

1. Why do you think Paul decided to do church plants with Priscilla and Aquila?
2. Why do you think God kept their names together in scripture?
3. What is your takeaway from the story of Priscilla?

Fill in the blanks (use the ESV translation):

Galatians 3:28. "There is neither Jew nor _____, there is neither _____ nor free, there is no male and female, for you are _____ in Christ Jesus."

Acts 18:18. "After this, Paul stayed many days longer and then took leave of the _____ and set sail for _____, and with him Priscilla and Aquila. At Cenchreae he had cut his hair, for he was under a _____."

Personal reflections:

If you are married, do you and your spouse serve the Lord together as a team?

_____

If you are not married, do you pray for a godly spouse? If not, why?

_____

_____

Write what a church planter is in your own words.

_____

_____

Write out Ecclesiastes 4:12.

_____

Lois and Eunice

Women who imparted the power of God's word

The names Lois and Eunice cannot be separated in the New Testament. They were used together by God for a greater purpose than just themselves.

They are mother and daughter. Eunice was Timothy's mother and Lois was his grandmother. Their names appear only once in the Bible, but—much like our own influence, which at times we think of as small—they had a lasting impact.

In the time of Paul's story (67 AD), Paul had finished his last letter to Timothy, his adopted spiritual son in the church. At the time there was nationwide persecution of the Christians under the reign of pagan Emperor Nero. He was an evil, ruthless emperor, the last in the Julio dynasty.

Paul fell victim to this persecution of the Christians and was imprisoned in the Coliseum in Rome, deep underground—a bit ironic, since he had once persecuted tho Christians. Sometimes we must live with the natural consequences of our sin even though we have been forgiven. *Read 2 Timothy 1:5.*

Read 2 Timothy 3:14–17. Paul knew his earthly time was coming to an end and wanted to pass on his mission to the next generation. Paul was convinced that the teachings would reach the nations and create a global revival. He knew the world needed the saving grace of Christ. *Read Acts 14:6–7.*

Paul had met Timothy twenty years before he wrote his final letter. He felt quickened in his spirit about Timothy's God-fearing character. Timothy's Christian teaching did not start with Paul, but rather with Timothy's mother and grandmother. Lois and Eunice had taught him from an early age. It was their teaching that was rooted and engrained in Timothy's heart. This is a great biblical example of reaping a harvest that others have sown. Paul reaped from the seed that Lois and Eunice had planted in Timothy as a boy. They taught Timothy so that one day he could preach the good news himself. Not knowing that was God's plan, they were led by the spirit. Timothy's name means "he that fears God" or "honors God."

Eunice was a God-fearing woman herself. However, she married an unsaved man and we do not know why. Maybe at the time these women had not surrendered to the Lord, or maybe the marriage was arranged by Eunice's father. The rest of the story of her marriage is unclear. But Timothy came from a mixed racial background. His mother was Jewish and his father was Greek.

We also do not know about Eunice's husband (Timothy's father) beyond that he was Greek. Did he die prematurely? The Bible does not say. We do know that Timothy was trained by Lois and Eunice in the holy scriptures from his earliest teaching. Likely they recalled the words of King Solomon: "Train up a child in the way he should go ..." (Proverbs 22:6 NIV). They valued the word and wanted Timothy to desire the daily bread and steadfast refreshment the word. The women led by example in Timothy's life. They were true believers, showing the fruit of Christ in their daily lives. This taught Timothy the foundation of the faith in which he went on to influence others for the very same thing.

Timothy got to see firsthand what that heart transformation looked like in action in the day-to-day events of life. We do know, however, that—although Lois and Eunice had deep faith in God and Jesus—their faith couldn't save Timothy. He had to choose to serve Christ on his own. *Read 1 Corinthians 4:16,17.*

Timothy heard the message in Lystra years prior when Paul was preaching there, and he dedicated his life to Jesus. He then activated his faith and became an apostle for Jesus. He spent his life sharing the good news of salvation. Paul used him greatly to help churches in Asia Minor and he joined Paul and Silas in preaching the gospel. Later, Paul granted Timothy written authorization to carry out his pastoral work in Ephesus. He did not get caught up in politics and never thought of the investment in younger Christians as a waste.

The obedience of Lois and Eunice prepared the soil that allowed the gospel message to take root in Timothy's heart so he would make the right choice for salvation. What greater inheritance could a mother and grandmother desire to offer but to see their children in heaven for eternity? We must heed their example and raise our children to know the ways of Jesus over the customs of this world. This world is fallen and belongs to Satan. If you raise a child to know the love of Christ, that forms a heavenly identity in them that cannot be shaken. *Read Acts 16:1–2.*

Verses about Lois and Eunice:

- ➤ Proverbs 22:6
- ➤ Isaiah 55:11
- ➤ Daniel 12:3
- ➤ Acts 16:31
- ➤ 1 Corinthians 4:15, 17; 15:1–4
- ➤ 2 Corinthians 5:20
- ➤ 1 Timothy 1:15
- ➤ 2 Timothy 1:2, 5, 9; 4:7–8; 2:2; 14:6–7; 4:5, 9
- ➤ 1 Peter 1:23

Questions about Lois and Eunice:

1. List two ways Timothy was influenced by his mother and grandmother.
2. How does scripture prepare us for God's service or the mission field?
3. How did God bless their godly obedience in raising Timothy?
4. How did their teaching prepare him for ministry?

Fill in the blanks (use the ESV translation):

1 Timothy 1:1–2. "Paul, an apostle of Christ Jesus by _____ of God our Savior and of Christ Jesus our hope. To Timothy, my true _____ in the _____: Grace, mercy, and peace from God the Father and Christ Jesus our Lord."

1 Timothy 1:18. "This charge I entrust to you, Timothy, my child, in accordance with the _____ previously made about you, that by them you may _____ the good _____."

Personal reflections:

Have you been asked to do something by the Lord but did not obey? What were the consequences?

_____

_____

Were you raised by godly parents? If not, what has influenced you most in a godly way?

_____

_____

What was something God was preparing you for that at the time you did not realize, but now are grateful He was faithful?

_____

_____

_____

Write out 2 Timothy 3:16–17.

_____

_____

Week Eight Review

Review your Bible verses for each woman. Pray over new revelation through the word.

Weekly Challenge:

Ask God to help you speak life over every person and situation you face this week, including speaking life over yourself.

Prayer:

Heavenly Father, I come before You knowing Your mercies are new every morning. I know there are times I fail You and do not put You first, and I repent from that. I desire Your way, Your will, and Your desires for my life. I give You permission to open and close doors that are in alignment with Your will for my life. I will stand firm knowing I trust You and find peace abiding in the vine. Jesus, You are my source, my joy, and my strength. Not just in time of need but in every day and all situations I face, I will call upon You and respond how Jesus would. Help me to become more like Christ, to choose a heavenly perspective, and to pick up my cross for Jesus every day. Give me the mind of Christ and the heart to love others with great mercy as You do for me. I pray this in Jesus's mighty name, amen.

Weekly Declaration:

I declare that I will embrace that I am perfectly and wonderfully made by God. I will not focus on my imperfections and flaws but see them as unique things that set me apart as His master creation. I will not criticize myself or compare or compete against others. I will love how I was made and do not question the potter's vision. This is my declaration.

Conclusion

From the pages of Genesis to the New Testament gospels we have seen a thread woven throughout the study of God's *faithfulness*. In His commitment to us as His children, He never stops teaching us through experience and discipline how to live righteously. From the story of Hagar to that Mary of Jerusalem we see God how steps into our circumstances and is faithful to provide a way.

"Your steadfast love, Oh Lord, extends to the heavens, your faithfulness to the clouds" (Psalm 36:5 ESV).

"The steadfast love of the Lord never ceases; His mercies never come to an end; they are new every morning; great is your faithfulness. The Lord is my portion, says my soul, therefore I will hope in Him" (Lamentations 3:22–24 ESV).

We witness this attribute of the Father many times through this study with perfect timing in each story. May we learn from these examples and endure in our faith until the end, replicating the faith.

When we fail through sin, we can come to Jesus for *forgiveness* and offer Him our repentance. We can be assured it will never be rejected. He is just and wants to forgive when we veer off the path He planned for us. We see this example in the life of Bathsheba and how her repentance brought restoration to her life and a lineage of hope.

"If we confess our sins, He is faithful and just and will forgive us our sins and cleanse us from all unrighteousness" (1 John 1:9 ESV).

True biblical repentance is the key to a healthy, fruitful relationship with Jesus. In and through Him we are made righteous, and only by Him. We can learn from the women who were vulnerable before the Lord and walked in humility to repent for their sins. God was faithful to heal them, redeem them, or open new doors. As long as we live a lifestyle of repentance, we are after the Father's heart.

Another major thread we can see through this study are the *promises* of God being heard and fulfilled through the obedience of the saints. Once we offer our hearts in surrender, the Lord can move mightily in our lives, completing promises spoken over our lives. We can see this so evidently in the promises of Leah and Hannah for a child. God heard their prayers and was able to open their wombs to receive the gift of motherhood.

The Lord desires to bless us even more than we desire to be blessed, the Bible says. If we could fathom the depth of God's love for us, we would stand in amazement. The promises and words spoken over our lives stay dormant if we do not access faith. Like the Bible mentions, faith without works is dead. If we partner in our faith with the Lord, we will see the promises and desires come to pass in our own lives much like the women we have studied. Let that be an encouragement to your spirit. The Bible says the prayers of the righteous rise like incense that is pleasing to the Lord (Psalm 141:2 NIV).

"And blessed is she who believe that there would be a fulfillment of what was spoken to her from the Lord" (Luke 1:45 ESV).

"He who calls you is faithful; He will surely do it" (1 Thessalonians 5:24 ESV).

We can trust the Lord to complete the work He started within our hearts and lives. This is a major testimony for the women studied and we can see such victory in their stories and have hope for our own.

Lastly, we can see God's provision through these women's lives while He *positions* them for greatness. He is the ultimate qualifier. The Bible says many are called but few are chosen. God does not call the qualified; rather, He will qualify the called. We do not have to rely on our strength and capacity, but God's infinite source that never runs dry.

We can see the testimony of God's position in Esther, Deborah, Mary of Jerusalem, and Lois and Eunice in great detail. He used them in perfect timing for a particular way that moved history forward. Whether it was positioned by a king, positioned in battle, positioned to have a home church during a time of the persecuted church, or positioned to raise a leader, God moved.

As we study the lives and stories of the word we can see God's way of positioning obedient people to further His will and destiny for mankind. He did this with His son, Jesus. He positioned Him in a time in history to die for the sins of all mankind, thus justifying the law and fulfilling all prophesies. It is the greatest example we have to see how God's positioning along with our obedience can accomplish great things for His glory.

"I am reminded of your sincere faith, a faith that's has dwelt first in your grandmother Lois and in your mother Eunice and now, I'm sure, dwells in you as well" (2 Timothy 2:5 ESV).

We can trust the Lord always. His love for us endures forever. During the journey of this eight-week study, I hope that you have learned many things about these women as well as about yourself. As you completed the personal reflection questions, your honesty with yourself and God has brought you closer.

Glossary

Omnipotent All-powerful, overseeing all of creation

Omnipresent Everywhere at once, referring to God's power and presence

Gentile Not Jewish or of the chosen people of Israel

Nazarite Dedicated to God in the womb for His works; a person holy unto God who must abstain from drinking wine and touching the dead and cutting their hair

Supernatural The unseen realm that God and the angels work in; if you have the "seeing gift" you can see into this realm

Covenant A promise with God (The Old Covenant was with Moses, and the New Covenant came when Jesus went to the cross. This no longer requires circumcision of the body, but now takes place in the heart.)

Kinsman redeemer The closest relative, who has the authority and duty to redeem the rights of another or avenge his wrongs

Book of Life God's book of every righteous deed and person who is saved through Jesus

Book of Death Every unrighteous deed of the people destined for separation from God in hell

Intercession The act of praying for someone on behalf of oneself or others

Idol An image or representation of a god used for worship

Concubine A woman who lives with a man but has a lower status than his wife

Imprecatory Psalms Psalms that invoke judgment, calamity, or curses upon an enemy who's perceived as the enemy of God

Divine intervention The intervention of God in the situation for His divine reasons

NOTES

NOTES

NOTES

NOTES

About the Author

Melissa Joy Parcels lives in Calgary, Canada, with her husband Ryan and young son Kesler. She owns and operates a successful dental hygiene clinic and founded a private vocational dental college in Calgary Alberta.

She is a lover of Jesus and His perfect message of salvation for the lost. She is committed to teaching new believers the word through her unique style. She launched Jeremiah Fire Ministries, a teaching ministry, in 2019. Jeremiah Fire hosts live and online bible studies, classes, and home studies. Jeremiah Fire's primary mission is to teach the Bible truths and stories to believers to grow their relationship with Christ.

Melissa has written several books and Bible curriculums, teaching leaders all over the globe. She has the heart to see people live out their God-given destinies.